Catwalk Crazy

Kelly McKain

USBORNE

My
<u>totally</u> secret
journal
by

Lucy Jessica Hartley

Saturday the 24th of September

𝓗i girls! It's Lucy Jessica Hartley here with another totally fab and *utterly shushingly* secret journal. Not much has been happening since we went back to school, but luckily I have just had the most amazing *Creative Inspiration* and my life is about to become massively Interesting with a capital "I" and "Exciting" with a capital E.

But before I reveal my *Creative Inspiration*, I will quickly catch you up on what's been going on in my life for the past few weeks. Sadly my fab tan from the summer (which I mainly got when me, Jules and Tilda went on holiday together!) has almost gone and I am nearly back to looking pastily English instead of from somewhere like LA where everyone is constantly brown. It's still a bit hot sometimes at school and if the sun does come out at break we all sit in a row on some of the benches with our legs sticking out, to try and get some more tan before it's too late, like:

Me!

Tilda's second name is Van der Zwan because of her dad being Dutch. Her mum is English but she died when Tilda was little. (Poor T!)

Jules's proper name is Julietta Garcia Perez Benedicionatorio, but no one calls her that 'cos it would take too long, especially if it was an emergency

Er, what else has been happening since I wrote my last journal? Well, virtually *nada*, as Jules would say 'cos of her Spanishness. I have worn in my new uniform stuff so it doesn't look as geeky and Back To School any more. And of course, I am still ⭐ **13** ⭐ which I became over the summer and which is *teen-tastic*!

And that is literally IT apart from the usual of eating, sleeping, watching *Friends* on E4 and arguing with Alex (I'm sure you know who he is by now – i.e. my little bro, who is 90% annoying but actually 10% okayish). Lately we have been mostly arguing about whose turn it is to sit in the front seat on the way to school and whether we are getting a cat or a dog. (I am saying cat and he is saying dog – and Mum is saying, "You're not having a pet, there's enough hard work and mess round here as it is!")

Please don't think from reading that bit that my mum is this mega-grumpy pet-stingy-pants, 'cos she is actually really nice. She just has loads to do because of having to bring me and Alex up as a single parent since Dad **CRUELLY ABANDONED** us, erm, about 8 months, 9 months…oh wow,

I have just worked out it was a whole year ago.
I never thought I'd feel better about it, especially
when Mum and Dad were doing their thing of
arguing all the time, but I don't mind so much
now, 'cos they are getting on better and me and
Alex get to see Dad a lot anyway 'cos he lives in
town (with his brother, our Uncle Ken, in this
manky flat that smells of curry and feet – yurgh!).

Actually I feel a bit strange writing how Dad
CRUELLY ABANDONED us in capital letters now. I
used to write it all the time, but now it seems a bit
like I am being mean to him when he had to leave
because of being really unhappy. Oh course, he is
still a big idiot for not working it out with Mum or
trying to make any effort *whatsoever*, but
somehow it doesn't feel as bad now. In fact I might
go back and cross out what I just wrote in capitals,
but actually then I would have a big smudge in my
lovely new journal, so maybe not.

Oh, yes, I have suddenly remembered the
reason why I was starting a new journal in the first

place! Oh, dear, I am so bad at going off the point (or maybe I am good at it!).

Well, guess what?!

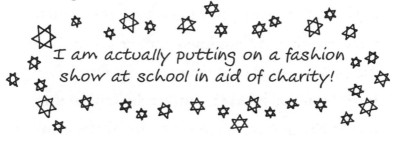

I am actually putting on a fashion show at school in aid of charity!

I know you are thinking, Lucy Jessica Hartley, surely that is impossible, but...

Yes! Really! It is 100% true!

What happened was, yesterday morning I was just quickly mentioning to Mum how it wasn't fair that we are only allowed Coco Pops on the weekend and how in the week we have to have Boring Hamster Bedding cereal from the health shop. (I call it that because it looks like shredded loo rolls and wood shavings – and tastes like them too!

Not that I know what shredded loo rolls and wood shavings taste like, but the **BHB** is how I imagine them.) When I said how deprived I am, Mum suddenly got annoyed for no reason and waved this little supplement thing she'd got out of the paper at me. "Honestly, Lucy, you don't know you're born!" she said all huffily, which is weird because *obviously* I do know I'm born, or how would I be here on this planet of earth? Anyway, she put the supplement thingie down on the table in front of my boring breakfast and flounced off upstairs.

Well, I started having a flick through, because it was taking forever to chew the **BHB** cereal, and it was about this charity that helps deprived children all around the world. I was reading about how you can buy a goat for a child for £24 and at first I was thinking, *Why would anyone want a goat, is it some weird kind of pet?* and also, *How unfair that some kids get a goat when I haven't even got so much as a goldfish?* But then when I started reading it properly (while *still* chewing) I found out that loads of kids don't have enough proper food, not even of the **BHB** cereal variety, and that giving them a goat can help them have milk and cheese and butter and all the stuff that we take for granted is in the fridge, or even if you run out it is always in Sainsbury's.

I started looking at the other things you can buy too, like a library full of books for kids who don't have one in their school. (I mean, no books! How awful would that be??) That is mega-expensive, almost £500, but still, there are loads of other things. Like, did you know that some kids don't even get the chance to go to school and you can give someone a scholarship for three years for about £250? I know school is sometimes annoying, especially when you're busy doing your own things in the loos like trying on make-up and then the bell rings and lessons get in the way. Plus, school is also annoying 'cos of teachers like Mr. Cain the *School Uniform Police*, who is campaigning for us to all wear straw boaters (these weird kind of hats) and long socks and be like Victorian young ladies. Being as how I am the *Queen of Style*, he is utterly my arch-enemy. But Mr. Cain is only one tiny bad thing, and if there were no schools there would be no reading and writing and art and maths and that, which is everything I need to know to run my own business as a *Real Actual Fashion Designer* (which is my Life's Ambition, **BTW**). I thought of all the kids who might want to be *Real Actual Fashion Designers* for their Life's Ambition but wouldn't be able to 'cos of not going to school, and suddenly I knew why Mum got annoyed and I felt really bad for saying I was deprived for having to eat the **BHB** cereal (it is still gross, though!). Plus, I wanted to do something to help the deprived kids be able to go to school and have libraries and also goats.

But then I was thinking, how am I possibly going to get £24 for even *one* goat? I knew I could never get it all on my own. For example, as soon as

Mum gives me my £10 pocket money it is all mysteriously gone in about one morning when I have only just bought some eyeshadow and a bracelet from Beaujangles and had a hot chocolate down at Cool Cats café with my **BFF**, and...

Sorry, I have gone off the point again!

So going back to the deprived children and the goats and everything, I was suddenly struck with the *Creative Inspiration*. As Mum came galloping down the stairs telling me and Alex to get in the car or we'd be late for school I yelled out, "I could put on a fashion show to raise money for Oxfam!" ↰

That is the name of the goat-giving charity, BTW

Then suddenly all these ideas were coming to me at once and I had to grab the nearest bit of spare paper I could, which ended up being the phone pad, while getting bundled out of the door by Mum. I was so excited about my idea I forgot to go upstairs and put any mascara on – luckily I had a spare ~~tube wand~~ thingie (what *does* mascara come in??) in my bag, though. I didn't even fight for the front seat with Alex like normal but just jumped in the back and started scribbling down how—

Oh hang on.

My hand's already aching from writing all this, and I haven't even got to the main point yet. Not getting to the main point is this thing I do, like, all the time. Especially when I am thinking about stuff I want to buy from New Look. At the moment they have this lovely purple top that's got these lacy bits on the sleeve – oh, *eek*, I am doing it again!

I know, so that I get to the main point without any more distractedness, I will just stick my ideas I had for the fashion show in here instead of copying them out.

We could hold it in the main hall – fingers crossed Mr. Phillips agrees!

I could design the clothes myself

We'll have a casting for models like they do on Make Me A Su

I ran out of room, that is meant to say Supermodel, BTW

Mr. Cain won't be able to spoil it with his stricty sergeant major-ness 'cos it's in aid of charity

The Style School girls can do the make-up and hair and that!

Jules and Tilda can do it with me

BTW, in case you didn't read my totally secret journal called Style School, the style school girls are these Year 7s who are completely into fashion. We had a fab stall doing hair and make-up and nails at the school fayre so they are totally brill at all that stuff

I told Tilda and Jules about my idea when we were supposed to be doing English, and they thought it was coolio. Plus, 'cos they are fab **BFF** they came and knocked on Mr. Phillips the headmaster's office door with me at first break to ask.

Mr. Phillips is very tall with a booming voice and sometimes he is quite nice and fun and sometimes he is quite scary and strict, so you never know what you are going to get. When us three knocked, he called out, "Enter," and none of us wanted to go in first, because it sounded like he was in a scary-and-strict-type mood. So we all linked arms and entered at the same time, and he was just looking up at us from behind his desk and my mouth went completely dry like I had swallowed the Sahara desert and I was just doing that mouth opening and shutting thing that fish do. Luckily Jules poked me in the ribs and shoved me forward and that must have nudged my brain into gear because I started talking. I was like, "Sir, we have this cool idea of putting on a fashion show in the main hall and selling tickets for people to come to it and then giving all the money to Oxfam to buy goats for kids that don't have any, erm, goats and—"

I realized I was speaking at twice the normal speed, and my voice sounded like how a tape goes when the car stereo chews it up. Luckily Mr. Phillips smiled and told me to calm down and explain exactly how we intended to put on the show.

So I did, and Tilda added some useful bits about how much we could sell the tickets for and how many seats we were planning to have and that, and Jules did lots of *smiling encouragingly* to make him get subconsciously keen on the fashion show.

In the end he said, "It sounds like a good idea, girls, but I'll need to be sure that you really can pull it off. You'll have to keep me updated every step of the way."

All three of us were nodding and going "Yes, sir," and then he said…

"Okay, then, let's go for it. To start with, on Monday morning I'll need to see a detailed breakdown of the various tasks and who will be responsible for them, and a list of the help and equipment you'll need from the school."

So it was a **YES!!!!!!!!**

How cool is that?!

Then me and Jules and Tilda were walking backwards out of the door together and going, "Thank you, thank you, thank you," and when we got outside the office we had a big squealy hug in the corridor and then we all got mega-embarrassed 'cos Mr. P came out of his office behind us, so we walked quietly and sensibly into the girls' loos and had our big squealy hug there instead.

So on Monday we have got to show him all our official plans, so that is what I have been sorting out. Here is my list so far:

1. <u>Make-up and that</u> The Style School girls are going to be in charge of make-up and that, 'cos I asked them yesterday at lunch and they were mega-keen. They are doing these jobs:

Hair: Lizzie and Carla

Nails: Sunny

Make-up: ???

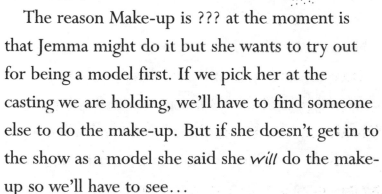

The reason Make-up is ??? at the moment is that Jemma might do it but she wants to try out for being a model first. If we pick her at the casting we are holding, we'll have to find someone else to do the make-up. But if she doesn't get in to the show as a model she said she *will* do the make-up so we'll have to see…

Jules and Tilda have said *yessity-yes-yes* to being in charge of the fashion show with me – how cool is that?! There are also some special jobs that we are doing ourselves or giving to other people, which are:

2. <u>Front of house</u> Tilda wanted to do something where she could put pencils in her hair

and go round with a clipboard so this is the perfect job for her. She will be the person taking tickets and showing people to their seats and to where the refreshments are on the night. That is great 'cos she's the best organizer I've ever met.

3. After-show Party Planner V. v. important

job! Jules is fab at planning parties 'cos her parents have one about every other Saturday. It's going to be at her house, and involve yummy Spanish food and cool music.

4. Technical Advisor Simon Driscott is going to

be this (I used to call SD the Prince of Pillockdom before I found out that he is a quite funny and okay boy and now we are sort of friends but with no fancying going on whatsoever). It means he's in charge of the lighting (i.e. what colours we are having flashing on and off, when and where the spotlights are going, etc.). The Geeky Minions, erm, whoops, sorry I mean the Charming Friends of Simon Driscott, are going to actually be putting the lights up where he says and that. (I am trying to remember not to call them the Geeky Minions now they are helping us.) When I've worked out what music I want to use, the ~~GMs~~ CFs of SD are going to be in charge of the sound too.

Actually, the Charming Friends of Simon Driscott weren't keen on joining in when I first asked 'cos they said fashion shows are girly and have nothing to do with a galaxy far, far away. But then Simon gave them their badges that he'd made specially on the computer (technologicality is his fave thing EVER).

So then the ~~Geeky Minions~~ Charming Friends decided to join in because the badges said "Engineer" on, and engineering is their fave thing because it involves technologicality *and* computers, plus you get to climb on the scaffold up to the sound and lighting rig. They are also building me a catwalk out of stage blocks, which they are happy about because **ALL** boys like Heavy Lifting, even the geeky ones.

5. *Producer* Me! That means I am putting the whole show together and deciding what the models should do and what music we're having. I am going to ask Mum if I can have a headset. The producer at Stella Boyd's fashion show had one and it was really cool 'cos you can organize people by speaking into it while doing other things at the same time with your hands, like whipping up a chocolate mousse or, erm,

basket weaving. **BTW**, Stella Boyd is this fab designer I met when I won a fantasy fashion comp and got to model my outfit down the catwalk in her actual fashion show!

6. _Designer_ Also me! I'm going to design all the outfits for the show. Of course, Jules and Tilda and the Style School girls are going to help me with the making as there will be loads to do. Not that I have even started _designing_ the outfits yet – gulp! – but still. We will have to use some already made things of course, but hopefully most of it can be from my original thinking. So I have got loads to do and you can see how it is **ABSOLUTELY VITAL** for me to have the headset.

7. _Head Seamstress_ Nan. Whoops, sorry, I mean _Delia_ – Nan doesn't like being _called_ Nan 'cos it makes her feel old! Anyway, she is being this 'cos she makes costumes for ballroom dancers for her job so she knows loads about making clothes and she has all the stuff.

And finally…

8. _Models_ Oh, dear we don't have any at the moment. We're holding a casting on Monday to get some. A casting is what you call an audition for models. I have watched it on _Make Me a Supermodel_, so I know. I think we need about six girls, and they can get changed once, and maybe two guys as well. Here's a miniature pic of the poster I did quickly yesterday lunchtime – Mr. Phillips let us make copies in the secretaries' office and we have stuck them up round the school, so hopefully we will get loads of wannabe catwalk stars coming along!

BE A MODEL!

We are looking for 6 girls and 2 boys to strut their stuff in our fab fashion show! Castings at 12:30 on Monday 26th in the hall. Confidence and attitude essential.

So that's on Monday and I completely can't wait! Jules and Tilda are coming round tomorrow to think of a theme for the fashion show, and we need to choose some music and decide how many seats we are having too, and make a cool ticket to photocopy and—

Yikes! I have suddenly realized that there are even more zillions and zillions of things to do than I'd thought! I'd better go and get started on poster designs and flick through some mags for theme ideas! Like, right now!

In fact there is not even enough time to write *byeeeeeeeeeeeeeeeeee*!!!!!!!!!!!!!!!! like I usually do. Oh, whoops I have written it anyway. *Argh!* Really REALLY got to go now!

Sunday morning, a new day is dawning.

How weird that I am rhyming for no reason.

I'm just waiting for Jules and Tilda to come round, so I decided to quickly write in here that I've been trying to choose the music for the fashion show. It's quite hard because it has to have a rhythm the models can walk to that's not too fast or too slow. I've been listening to loads of different things from the radio and the bit of Dad's CD collection that he hasn't taken with him to Manky Flat Land.

This morning I had the TV on E4 Music, with the living room door open, and I was seeing if any of the songs would be good by walking up and down the kitchen to them in a model-y way (you should give it a try – it's not as easy as you think!).

Mum came in and went, "Lucy, I hardly dare

even *ask* what you're doing." That's when I realized it probably did look a bit funny 'cos I was wearing my pyjamas and my special-occasion high heels.

When I explained about the music-choosing Mum put some heels on and joined in too, and soon we were collapsed in a big attack of giggles. "I think it's great that you're doing this," she said, when we'd got our breath back. "I wish there was some way I could be more involved."

That's really nice of her and I'm sure I'll think of something she can help with. Oh, that's the doorbell. Time to go *Catwalk Crazy*!!!

Sunday afternoon at 3.22 p.m. precisely

Jules and Tilda have just left and my head is buzzing with even more ideas!

Well, when Jules and Tilda came in (Tilda had already put some pencils in her hair in preparedness for our meeting) I made us some coffee and Jules had a cheese sandwich even though it was only about 10.30. We had coffee 'cos drinking it makes you go more businesslike, and we also had Wagon Wheels (not sure if they helped the businesslikeness but they were v. yummy!). Tilda was making notes of everything we said and instead of just saying, "What about this?" and, "What about that?" I was going, "What's the status on this?" and, "Can you give me an update report on the progress of that?" so it was really,

really businessy. In fact I wish I wore glasses, so that I could take them off and twizzle them round while talking business language.

Unfortunately Alex was being annoying by

A) existing, and
B) wanting to get involved,

so I had a good idea for getting rid of him. I said, "You're welcome to stay, darling bro, in fact we'll be trying out make-up looks in a minute so you can be the model."

Of course, he ran off going "Yuck!" and we were left in peace, beautiful peace!

First on our agenda of businesslikeness was to think of a theme for the show, so I did some shuffling of papers and we all reported our ideas for it.

Here's what we thought of:

1. Disco

2. Vampires (guess who thought of that!)
3. Pop stars
4. Film stars

Then we *Discussed The Options* and realized that if we had disco lights people might not be able to see the clothes that well and if we did film stars, we'd have to make gowns like the A-listers wear to premieres and stuff, and it would be too hard, plus not the sort of designs that people actually want to wear in normal life. I said no to vampires because I want it to be proper fashion and not dressing up like Halloween and Jules got all huffity and said, "I don't mean dressing up in a stupid costume, Lucy Jessica Hartley, but I mean, like, girls in cool mouldy ball gowns with ripped fishnet tights and fangs."

"Crypt chic," Tilda suggested.

"Exactly," said Jules, smiling at *her*, then folding her arms and glaring at *me*.

Attractive, ne c'est pas?

The problem with working with your **BFF** when you are actually in charge is that sometimes you have to say no to their ideas. I had to use all my subtleness to stop Jules getting in a *dark and stormy* mood with me, by going, "Well, of course the Crypt Chic idea is fabbity-fab-fab and just because I'm not choosing it doesn't mean the idea is not great and that you yourself are not great and also a fab **BFF**. We just need to pick something that most girls do, so that they can see the point of the fashion show, and most girls do not generally hang around in a graveyard in a mouldy ball gown."

Jules tried to keep looking cross but she joined in with the discussing after a while so I knew things were okay again between us.

So then we had some more theme ideas, which were:

1. Hanging out at the park
2. Shopping
3. Party

And it was cool 'cos we all liked all of those ideas, so suddenly out of nowhere we had three possible ones. We talked about them for a long time but we couldn't decide which was the best, so Tilda and Jules are leaving it to me to see if I come up with any designs that especially fit one idea or the other.

Then we had some lunch with Mum and Alex, which was tomato soup and cheese sandwiches, and we told them about our ideas for the themes. Alex thinks they are all cool too, but Mum is not that keen on "party" in case it is all tiny miniskirts (when she sees girls with really teeny-weeny ones on in town, she says, "Well, really, was it worth her even putting that *on*?") But of course the thought of getting to design cool miniskirts just made me like the idea of "party" even more!

After we'd helped with the clearing up and wangled a jam doughnut each, I showed Tilda and Jules the poster idea I had last night for the show.

Tilda is in charge of the front-of-house stuff, like I said, so it was up to her to *approve* the poster. She said it was great and just made a few tiny-weeny changes. Here is the final version (we will make it bigger on the photocopy, BTW):

GO CATWALK CRAZY!

Come to our fab fashion show

At: 4.30 p.m.

On: Friday 7th October

In: The hall, Tambridge High

Designs by Lucy Jessica Hartley

Tickets £3 from the School Office

All proceeds go to Oxfam

We have worked out that we can sell 62 tickets, as that's how many chairs we can get round the catwalk in two rows. Alex poked his nose in and asked if he could have a free ticket for being my brother, but I am being v. businesslike and making everyone buy them — after all, the more tickets we sell, the more goats we can get! Mum has helpfully bought three already (tickets, not goats, that is!) — for herself, Alex and her friend Gloria, I would guess. Oh hang on, Mum is calling me — just when I was talking about her. Spooky or what?

Hello, I am back again

For the last hour I have been doing my job of cleaning the bathroom (which I have to do for my pocket money). It only takes 21-ish minutes normally, but I got a bit involved in staring into the mirror experimenting with new ways of parting my hair, and then trying to decide if my top lip has recently gone thinner than normal, so it was more like 47 minutes in the end. When I'd finished I suddenly found myself deciding on the fashion show theme with no effort whatsoever. I realized that I don't fancy doing "hanging out in the park" because it is all baggy trousers and trainers and stuff and I want something a bit more girly and glam. I couldn't choose between the ideas of "shopping" and "party", so I have decided that the theme will be "shopping *then* party"!

When the models come down the catwalk the

36

first time, they'll be in their daytime shopping clothes, but carrying bags, as if they've just bought stuff to wear to a party that night. I can even reuse some of the stuff in their shopping outfits to show a daytime to evening look!

Plus, I can customize T-shirts for the boys and create a storyline where they're hanging out, watching the girls shopping and maybe fancying one. I have just texted this to Jules and Tilda and they think it is a fab idea *(phew!)* so that is one definite thing worked out! Yay! Now I just have to start having design ideas!

Oh, but first I have to go back to cleaning the bathroom because Mum has done her inspection and she reckons I've missed a bit round the sink. Urgh! I bet *Real Actual Fashion Designers* don't have to put up with this sort of thing!

Monday the 26th of September at 9.08 a.m.

(in registration – I have only just got here!)

Great news! I went to see Mr. Phillips before school and showed him all our plans, and he's really pleased. He let us photocopy some show posters in the school office, like he did with the *models wanted* ones, and plus he said we could miss registration while we went round sticking them up all over the school (which is cool 'cos usually the only okay excuse for missing registration is that you are in fact **DEAD**). Now the posters are up we can start selling massivo amounts of tickets, and hopefully we'll find some fab models later on today too! Oh, it is just so **FABULASTICALLY EXCITING!!!**

How annoying that the bell has just rung for our first lesson and I can't just stay here and plan fashion show stuff all morning! Gotta go!

12.14 p.m. after lunch

I am in the hall on my own
before the casting, just grabbing
some time to write something
v. v. secret in here.

I scoffed down my lunch in two minutes so I
could come in here first and get everything ready,
but it only actually took another two minutes to
set things up 'cos I just had to put three chairs out
behind a table for me and Jules and Tilda to be the
panel and that was basically it.

WARNING: The next bit is totally top secret and
something I absolutely cannot tell Jules or Tilda,
even though I normally tell them everything.

Oh dear, I am freaking out a bit, sort of standing up and sitting down and it's a bit like I've forgotten how to hold a pen. The thing is, I've realized that certain feelings have come back for a certain person who I used to fancy but who I honestly thought I didn't fancy any more. Okay, that is probably not helping you realize what I am going on about. I will have to spell it out, but in a code:

JJ no hsurc a tog llits evah I

Eeeeeeeekkkkkkkk!!!!

This morning me, Jules and Tilda were going round telling people about the casting. Mr. Phillips did an announcement about it in lower school assembly this morning so hopefully most people know, even if they haven't seen the posters, but we just wanted to make sure that the people we had our eye on as good models were coming.

So anyway, we all split up and went round the school telling people and I spotted Jules's older bro, JJ.

I just acted completely normal and asked him if he wanted to maybe audition to be one of the male models in our show, because at that point I didn't realize I still felt *you know what* about him. He shrugged his gorgeous shoulders and shoved his gorgeous hands in his gorgeous pockets. "Sure, why not?" he said. "It'll show Suzanna that I don't just sit in my room listening to music like *she* reckons. Not that I care what she thinks anyway."

I was in GOBSMACKED FLABBERGASTATION then, 'cos Suzanna is JJ's girlfriend and he's normally really nice about her. But it turns out that:

A) she is not his girlfriend any more 'cos she broke it off, and
B) he is all moody with her and doesn't want them to get back together even one iota

(which I think is like a tiny-weeny speck, like maybe as big as one of the little green bits on the end of a broccoli or something).

So when he said about not caring what she thinks, suddenly all my old feelings came rushing back and I was standing there completely tongue-tied and then even more suddenly I was the opposite of tongue-tied, which is gabbling embarrassingly about how I really want him to be involved in the fashion show because he'll get the upper school behind it as well and then I accidentally added, "and because of your gorgeously sultry Mediterranean looks" and my cheeks went so burning red I nearly SPONTANEOUSLY COMBUSTED right there in front of him, which is where you just suddenly burst into flames and after about 2 seconds only your shoes are left. Oh, sorry, there were no full stops at all in that bit. I hope you weren't reading it out loud. (Actually, I hope you weren't *anyway*, 'cos of it being **TOP SECRET**!)

JJ was looking at me quite weirdly by this time so I had to quickly think of an excuse to get away before I said anything even more embarrassing. But actually the excuse I came up with turned out to be even *more* embarrassing than the most embarrassing thing, 'cos I went, "Excuse me, but I have to go to the loo urgently."

I mean, criiiiiinge!!!!

Why couldn't I have said I need to make an urgent phone call or urgently find Jules and Tilda???????????????

So of course I had to go to the loo in case JJ suspected anything about my fancyingness of him and when I got there I just looked in the mirror to quickly check if my make-up had looked okay while I was talking to him. Then I got involved in trying to work out whether my left eye is actually higher up on my face that my right one, and I was in there so long that JJ probably thought I was doing a *you know what* (clue: *Numero Dos*).

CRINGE!!!!

Anyway, I just have to stop thinking about it now, 'cos I'm sure there's no way he would ever feel the same about me and the only place that this Return of the Killer Crush could possibly lead to is CRINGE-LAND!!!!!!!!!!

Oh good, I feel a bit calmer now I have got all that out. But don't forget that it is absolutely tippety-top secret. Jules mustn't find out how I feel 'cos she'd probably either:

A) think it was really funny and tell JJ and tease me in front of him and that, and then I would never be able to go round her house ever again, or

B) think it was really bad and annoying and get in a massive *dark and stormy* mood with me and that is the last thing I need when there is so much to do on the fashion show and

absolutely no time whatsoever for **BFF**
fallings out.

So I will just have to keep my burning red
cheeks under control when I see JJ at the casting
at 12.30. Which it nearly is, **BTW**.

Oh, yikes, here comes Jules, have to hide
this!!!!!!!!!

7.32 p.m.

I'm at home in my room, trying to get ideas for my designs, but I just wanted to quickly write in here and tell you what happened at the model casting first.

Well, basically, it was *soooooo* cool.

Simon Driscott brought his Polaroid camera along and took pix of everyone so that we could spread them out on the table afterwards and discuss them like they do on *Make Me A Supermodel*. 'Cos of it being his camera, we had to get an extra chair and let him join in the discussing bit, even though he knows absolutely zilchio about fashion (i.e. he still wears his tie in a kipper and thinks a duffel coat is the pinnacle of coolitude).

29 people turned up in the end (including JJ –

yay!), which was pretty good. They all signed their names on a form Tilda had made and then I did the welcome speech and explained about the fashion show being in aid of charity. Gina Fulcher turned up (she is this girl who was really nasty to Tilda when she first got here, so none of us like her 'cos we are **BFF** and we stick together on the not-liking of horrible bullies). While she was signing her name up on the form, Tilda did a Glance of Desperation at me, meaning, *Please, Lu, let's not have her in it*, and I tried to do psychicness back at her by saying loudly in my head, *Okay, we will most probably not have her in it, but we have to give her a fair chance with everyone else because of democracy.*

We got the Hopefuls to walk up and down in threes (and one 2 so that no one had to do it on their own) and luckily Gina didn't have any of the funky attitude and personality that we were looking for, so there was a professionalistic reason

47

for not picking her as well as a personal one. Jemma was really good, though, which I partly didn't want her to be 'cos of wanting her to do make-up, but mainly I was pleased for her. There were a few girls who were really fab and confident, including Liana Hawley from our class, and a couple who were a bit shy but who have cool looks.

While they were going up and down my mind was whirring about who would suit what sort of outfit and which girls and boys looked good walking down together, and I was conferring about this with Jules and Tilda. I want to have as many different looks and shapes and sizes as possible to make the fashion show interesting and like real life. I'm not into those shows when the girls all come out in the same make-up and they are all the same skinny shape and they all look like zombie clones.

After the Hopefuls had done the walking up and down I had the good idea of making an excuse to ask JJ's group to do it again, just so I could watch him and daydream about him being my boyfriend! He was a bit nervous and sort of shuffled along, but he is by 1 zillion % the most gorgeous of the boys.

When the Hopefuls had left, we spread all the Polaroids out on the table and did the panel discussion of deciding who we wanted to have in the show. Luckily we all pretty much agreed on the choices so it didn't take too long to discuss the models. Jemma is definitely in, so I will need to find a new make-up artist!

Because of Jules being there, I was careful to say JJ was only "okay" 'cos of not wanting her to be suspicious. It worked fabbly 'cos she got all *dark and stormy* about me not saying he was the most fab guy there, and she absolutely insisted on having him in the show. That was cool 'cos I got to look like I wasn't that bothered! The other guy we chose was Jamie Cousins from our class and for some reason Simon Driscott got a bit annoyed

49

when I kept saying how cool and confident and perfect for modelling he is.

The final choice of models is:

Freya

Liana

Jemma

Shamila

Bhavan

Megan

J.J

Jamie

I have drawn pretend Polaroid pictures because I am keeping the real ones for showing Nan (as in Delia) when we're planning the designs.

After school we got all the Hopefuls back together in the hall to do the announcement of who was being in the show. I said how everyone was good in their own way and I explained that 'cos we want all different looks we had to choose some people and not others, so hopefully no one minded not getting in, and then I announced the names.

Then the ones who weren't being in it said well done to the ones that were (except Gina Fulcher, who said, "It's a stupid fashion show and I never wanted to be in it anyway!" and stormed off). I asked our chosen models to bring in a pair of jeans or casual skirt each that they wouldn't mind me customizing for the show. I also said how we'd be doing a catwalk workshop tomorrow so we could practise the walking and think about poses and stuff. Megan and Shamila are a bit shy so I want to start working with them as soon as poss so there's plenty of time for them to come out of their shells, like:

After school me and Jules and Tilda went to check with the secretaries and we haven't sold many tickets so far (like, only 8!). But then, we haven't been trying massively hard to advertise 'cos of being so busy with other stuff. There's still loads of time though so I'm not too worried.

On the way home I went into New Look and Beaujangles (this really cool accessories shop in town) for inspiration for my designs. We have now got models but at this rate there'll be nothing for them to wear! I also bought the *Hey Girls! Fashion Special*, which is packed with top style tips and hopefully it will give me loads of fab ideas for the designs. I'm off to look through it now (and to have another look at the Polaroid of JJ!).

Byeeeeeeeeeeeeeeeeeeee!

Tuesday at 4.15 p.m.,
sitting at the kitchen
table writing this!

I learned from *Real Actual Fashion Designer* Stella Boyd that it's important to call everyone sweetie and darling all the time when you're doing a catwalk show (it adds to the atmosphere) so I decided to start this morning. When I did it to Mum she just gave me a funny look but when Alex came down and I went, "Morning, darling, mwah, mwah!" he just stared at me in utter confusion and went, "Don't you mean, 'Oi, toad face, did you scoff all the Fromage Frais tubes?'"

(Charming! As if I am ever that mean to him!)

The model training went really well (well, really, *really* well in one secret way which I will tell you in a mo). Luckily I have been glued to

54

Make Me A Supermodel – well, not actually glued like this:

but in the way of keenly watching every episode, so I knew what kind of comments to say during the catwalk practice.

So once everyone was there, including Jules and Tilda, Simon put the music on (I picked out three good songs the other night) and then I showed the models how to do the walk, which you wouldn't think is that hard but actually it can be tricky when there are loads of people staring at you. What you do is come down the catwalk in a sort of posh way with your shoulders back, standing up really straight and looking ahead of you instead of down at your feet like most people tend to do when they are just walking normally. Then at the end you stop so the photographers can take pix of you and you sort of go, *hip, hip, head,* which means you sort of stick out your hip, then your other hip, and then you turn your head like you're trying to see something v. quick shoot behind your right shoulder. Then you might want to take off your jacket and do a swinging the jacket thing before walking back. (We will just have one photographer in fact, i.e. Simon Driscott, who has got a really cool digital camera, which he used when we did our fashion shoot for the school mag.)

I have noticed that on the catwalks in America (which are actually called runways over there, **BTW**, like we have for aeroplanes) the models do this weird walk where their knees come up really high, as if they're stepping between giant cowpats, like:

I did a demonstration of it and explained to our models how I didn't want them to look like that, but not as if they were just walking down the road either, but somewhere in between.

I got the girls to have a go and I was saying the *hip, hip, head* thing when they got to the end. They kept giggling at first but after a while they got a bit more professionalistic and forgot how silly they felt having to model in their gross-o-matic school uniforms which no way in a zillion years would ever be in a fashion show! But after a few tries on their own and in twos they were getting it more right. Jemma was *soooooo* good and Shamila was much less shy. When I said how good Megan was she was really pleased and told me she'd been practising going up and down the hallway at home.

After a few more goes, I said well done to the girls and also that every chance they get they all have to practise walking very straight with their shoulders back. (They were all giggling because when you do that your you-know-whats stick forward!)

When the boy models did their walk, JJ was even more nervous than before. I was surprised 'cos I thought he'd be confident now he's seen what to do. But maybe it didn't help that he was stuck in a room of girls all giggling about their you-know-whats sticking forward! He sort of shuffled along looking at the floor and when he tried to do the jacket swinging thing with his blazer he got sort of half trapped inside it and was flailing about going more and more red and when he finally escaped from it he almost *ran* back up the pretend catwalk, not in time to the music at all.

Oops! V. soz, I have forgotten about full stops again. Here are a few to make up for it. . . ..

So then JJ did it again and he was still a bundle of nervosity. When he got to the end of the catwalk I went and showed him how to stand for the posing bit and I put my arm round his waist to move him into the right position. I just did it in a really professionalistic way without thinking and then I suddenly realized **WHAT** I was exactly doing and I was like:

I wanted to move my arm before I went bright red, but then I also wanted to leave it there for like, ~~5 mins~~ ~~half an hour~~ ~~one day~~ FOREVER. Because of the strain of thinking two opposite things at once my brain had a meltdown and I ended up just sort of stuck there. After what felt like about 2 years but was probably only about 10 seconds I had to actually lift my arm off with my other hand, and mumble something about how it must have gone to sleep there – CRINGE!

But just then Jamie Cousins, the other guy model, asked me a question and then I made sure to adjust his position too so it looked fair and equal and Jules would not suspect any fancyingness of JJ by me and would believe the hand-falling-asleep excuse.

So I think I got away with that one – *phew!*

Talking of my fancyingness of JJ *(shhh!)* I did have a really good idea of how we could spend some time together without anyone else around. When the bell went and everyone hurried off to class I went up to him and gabbled, "How about I give you some extra practice, one-to-one without the girls here so that you can get over your nerves and also be able to concentrate without them giggling about their you-know-whats sticking forward?"

I went bright red then, **OBVIOUSLY.** Y-O-Y-O-Y-O-Y do I always have to start mentioning *embarrassing things* as soon as I talk to him?! Urgh! Anyway, luckily while I was busy DYING of embarrassment he said, "Yeah, okay, that would be cool," and left.

So, how fab is that? I've got a chance to spend some time alone with him, even if he doesn't know I'm thinking of it like that!

HA-HA-HAAAAAA!!!!

Evil-genius laugh!

7.12 p.m.

I've just been through all the stuff the models brought in at lunchtime...

... and there are some fab things.

Thank goodness Tilda the Organized reminded me to get them to put their initials on the labels so I would know whose was whose. I can take their sizes from these for the things I'm going to make from actual scratch too.

I've pulled out all my sketchbooks of designs that I've done so far and my inspiration books of cuttings from mags, and all my jewellery and accessories, and I'm just going to have a massive blitz of thinking what I can do for each outfit. I especially like a miniskirt with footless tights that I saw in the *Hey Girls! Fashion Special*, and this thing of layering different tops so you have loads of straps, so I'm going to try and use those ideas in my designs.

I'm going to Nan-as-in-Delia's house tomorrow night so I want to have all 14 ideas to show her and then she can tell me what I might have to change and what we can manage to do in the time. Even with all the helpers it is going to be quite tricky to get it all done.

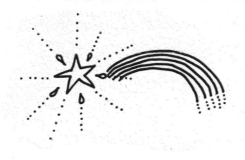

Wednesday after school

I'm just going to stick all my new design stuff in here for safety, 'cos it is on all different bits of paper. I have been designing stuff all day (getting all the inspiration last night really helped) so I haven't got much work done in the lessons. Oh, well, I'll have to catch up after the fashion show is over!

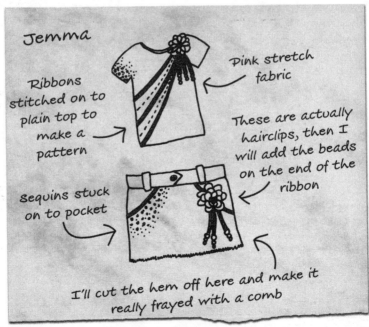

Jemma

Pink stretch fabric

Ribbons stitched on to plain top to make a pattern

These are actually hairclips, then I will add the beads on the end of the ribbon

sequins stuck on to pocket

I'll cut the hem off here and make it really frayed with a comb

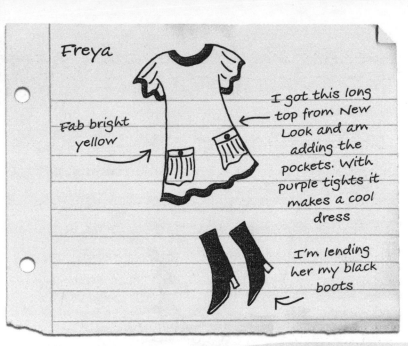

Freya

Fab bright yellow

I got this long top from New Look and am adding the pockets. With purple tights it makes a cool dress

I'm lending her my black boots

Shamila

Liana

Purple

This top will be made from scratch – I chose the material and Nan will help loads

Red with dots

I'll make a simple denim skirt like the one I saw in the Hey Girls! Fashion Special

65

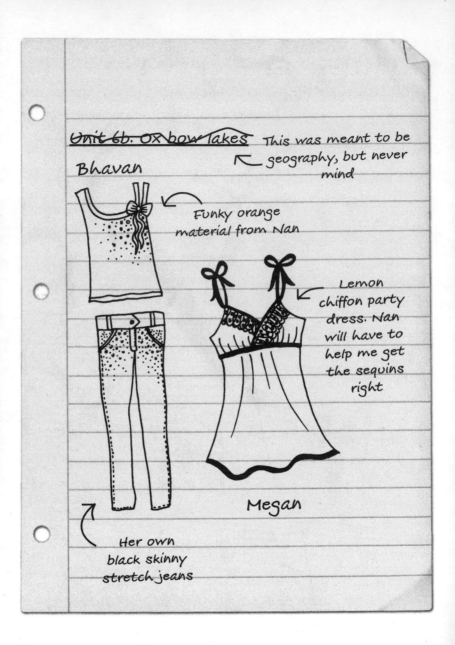

Unit 6b. Oxbow lakes This was meant to be geography, but never mind

Bhavan

Funky orange material from Nan

Lemon chiffon party dress. Nan will have to help me get the sequins right

Megan

Her own black skinny stretch jeans

I have just about got all my ideas, at least in rough. I can't wait to see what Nan-Delia thinks tonight!

I have got up an hour early to get ready for school 'cos I'm doing one to one model training with JJ today and I want to look as fab as poss!

I just wanted to quickly tell you that it went really well with Nan (Delia) last night. She loved my design ideas and made loads of really helpful suggestions about how I could change some of them a bit so it's easier to make them, and also she had some fab material that I wanted to use as well.

So when we'd agreed on the changes we drew all the designs out as final finished ideas and then stuck the fabric swatches and sequins and beads around each picture so that you can see all the textures and colours too. They look *soooooo* amazing I can hardly believe they have come from my own head. Nan has kept half the finished pictures to work from, but I have brought the other ones home 'cos I am in charge of putting the accessories together. Here's what I've found so far:

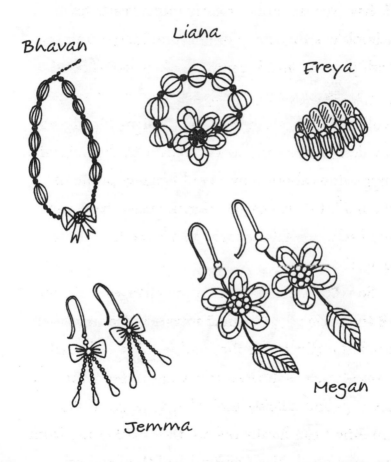

Bhavan

Liana

Freya

Jemma

Megan

I am also in charge of customizing the T-shirts for the boy models (including JJ – yay!) because I have got my T-shirt printing kit. For the party we're going to reveal the T-shirts after having them under jackets and scarves for the shopping bit. My ideas are:

JJ

Frayed panel printed with a pattern and sewn onto the T-shirt

Red

White

Silver

Same on arm

Jamie Cousins

Gold printed pattern

Black

Two T-shirts inside each other. One neckline cut away to show other

Red frayed sleeves from old T sewn on

Last night Nan made a list of what extra things we need to buy, and she is getting the stuff and paying, which is massively nice of her. I did all the saying of "Are you sure?" that you do to be polite but she is insisting. She says she's happy to do it because it's for charity, so none of our goat-buying money will have to go into spending out for materials. Plus, we are getting together for a Design and Production Meeting tomorrow night before the massive making session on Saturday round hers. How professionalistic is that?!

Oh, I have just seen the time. I have to go now 'cos I've only got 40 minutes left to do my make-up. I'm doing the Natural Look so that Mr. Cain doesn't make me wipe it off before lunchtime, and plus I am taking some cool purple lacy tights and some bracelets and lipgloss to put on quickly just before I see JJ after any Mr. Cain danger has passed.

Wish me luck!

Thursday at home,
surrounded by all my
fashion show design stuff.

I have to get on with all this in a sec, but my mind is whirling round and round with JJ stuff and if I don't just write it down I will never be able to concentrate!

During the extra modelling practice JJ and I did the walk down where the catwalk will be (like he might have to do with one of the girl models). In fact we did it about 8 times. That was about 6 more times than we needed to, but I just really liked walking arm in arm with him and by the end I had completely forgotten we were doing it for the fashion show and I had started imagining that there was a vicar at the end of the catwalk and it was in fact for our

wedding!!!

Oops, sorry – I got a bit carried away with sketching that!

JJ has improved a bit modelling-wise, but he's still v. v. nervous and I had to keep reminding him to look up and not at his feet all the time.

Afterwards we sat down on the stage bit at the end of the hall, kind of half behind the curtain, and I said some *Constructive Criticism* about his walk instead of blurting out something embarrassing like I usually do – phew!

Then JJ said, "I think it's brilliant that you're doing all this for charity, Lu. You're not just a pretty face, are you?"

My eyes were popping out with JOY then 'cos I was thinking, *That must mean he thinks I am a pretty face AS WELL*. So then I tried to look more pretty, by turning my head round so he could see my left side, which I have worked out is my best. But then he was looking so puzzledly at me that I just had to go back to facing forward normally.

Then I gathered up all my bits of courage and said, "So, are you feeling okay about the break-up now?" like I was only concerned as a friend.

"Yeah, it's like, whatever, I'm totally over it. I mean, like, Suzanna who? You know what I'm saying. It's history," he muttered, and I had to stop myself from leaping up and going "Hurrah!!!" And then he said **AN AMAZING THING**, which was, "In fact, I sorta kinda like someone else."

And then he said an **EVEN MORE AMAZING THING**. If I write it in here you have to swear to keep it absolutely tippety-top secret, because if Jules found out she would kill me into pulverized deadness with either cringe-making teasing or *dark and storminess*. He said:

I was going to like, kind of, maybe ask you out?

Even before I could think about acting cool, I found myself yelling "Yes!" really loudly and punching the air, like my dad does when Man U score a goal. By the time I remembered not to embarrass myself, it was way too late. Urgh!

But luckily JJ was smiling and he started leaning

75

forward and I thought maybe he was about to kiss me and I started wondering if I had overdone my lipgloss and if maybe our lips would just go sliding off each other, but I didn't have the chance to find out because someone poked their head round the curtain and we both sprang up in a massive hurry. I went, "So, this is where you'll be starting from, and then you walk out through the curtain and onto the catwalk and that's it. Any questions?"

"Erm, no," JJ mumbled, and then he muttered something about getting a drink and hurried off, so I was left there with the person who had interrupted us, just thinking, *Phew, thank goodness it is not Jules,* and trying to look like something **AMAZING** had not just happened.

BTW, the interruptive person was Simon Driscott. He looked kind of pale for some reason, even more than usually, and usually he is pale as a sheet (a white sheet, obviously!) 'cos of spending all his time in the computer room.

"I thought you might be in here," he said. "I

just came to ask you about the coloured gels for the lights. Did you want a light pink and then the deep rosy one or can we just use one pink and then move straight onto the purple?"

"Oh, erm, one pink is fine, yes, good idea," I said and bolted out of the hall.

So now I am really happy but also a bit confused. I didn't see JJ for the rest of the day so I don't know if:

A) he was asking me out,
    or
B) he was just asking if he *could* ask me out.

So that means I don't know if he thought I was saying:

C) "Yes, I will go out with you,"
    or
D) "Yes, you can ask me out sometime, that would be okay."

Obviously *I* know what I meant, i.e. "Yes, yes, *yeeeeeeeeeeeess*, I will *soooooo* be your girlfriend!" but whether JJ knows that depends on what he meant in the first place, if you get what I mean.

Of course, there's no way I can actually *ask* him what he meant, 'cos, like, how CRINGE-MAKINGLY UNCOOL would that look?

I suppose I'll just have to see what happens.

I also wish I could talk to someone about it, but I can't tell Jules. I can't tell Tilda either, even though I am *desperate* to because, as you know, if you tell one of your BFF something and not the other it leads to *Scary Trouble of the Falling Out Kind.*

So I'm stuck with my asking out confusion, which will be called Asking Out Confusion from now on, or even AOC if I have to write it quickly.

By teatime I was so bursting to tell someone about the AOC that I tried to talk to Mum about it, but she didn't entirely get what I was on about. I started off going, "Mum, you know when you like someone, you know, like as in LIKE them, and then you don't like them and you really think the feeling of liking them has gone away but then it, like, comes back again?"

Mum looked a bit startled and stopped stirring the Moroccan Lamb Tagine (which is one of the exotic things she likes making – I find it weird because it has apricots in when it is not pudding).

"Why? What's he told you?" she said.

"Who?" I went, confusedly.

"No one," she said quickly, and carried on stirring. I was going to ask what she was talking about but then she said, "I just meant, whoever he is, I hope he's not an older boy again, Lucy, like when you got sweet on that Wayne Roman from the boy band…"

"*Yurgh*, Wayne Roman is gross, and *double yurgh*, no one says 'sweet on', that's *soooooo* icky, we say, 'Do you fancy him?' or even 'Do you want to snog him?'" I patiently explained.

"You haven't been kissing a boy, I hope!" Mum

totally shrieked. "Lucy, it says in my book, *Raising Teenagers: The Most Rewarding Years* that—"

"No I have **NOT**!" I squealed interruptingly back to her. "I just mean that's what we teenagers generally say!"

And then I realized that telling Mum about JJ would only make her worried, especially seeing as he actually *is* an *older boy* and also because I *am* maybe about to *snog him* in the near present. So then I said, "Anyway, I wasn't talking about *me* liking a boy but just about this girl in my class who you don't even know liking a boy." Mum still did eyebrow-raising at me but then I subtly changed the subject to the fashion show and told her all about how it was going.

When I got on to the problem of still needing a make-up artist because Jemma is now being one of the models, Mum said, "Have you got anyone in mind?"

"No," I said, "or I would just simply ask them, wouldn't I?"

She put the lid on the casserole dish and leaned back against the counter, going, "Lucy, can you really think of no one who loves make-up, has all the kit and would really like to be involved in your show?"

"No, or I wouldn't be worrying about it!" I said calmly and sensibly (well, okay, more like crossly and snappily). You have to repeat things a lot when Mum's been at work all day, 'cos she gets tired and her listening skills evaporate.

She sighed. "So you can think of no one who might let you use her **MAC** collection?"

And that's when the realization dawned on me and I cried, "You!"

"Well done!" said Mum. "Really, Lucy, I sometimes wonder what planet you're on! I'll ask for next Friday afternoon off then."

I said thanks and gave her a big hug. Then I gave her a helpful tip by going, "Mum, you should have just clearly said what you meant in the first place so that there could be no confusion. In fact, people should even write things down so that no one can possibly ever get confused about whether other people mean A or B or C or D."

"Sorry, love, I don't follow," she said then and I had to quickly say, "Oh nothing," and then zip my lips in case any more JJ stuff came out by itself.

Oh, I wish I could just give JJ a form like this:

Please tick the relevant box:

☐ I am going out with Lucy Jessica Hartley.

☐ I am thinking of maybe asking out Lucy Jessica Hartley sometime in the nearly current future.

Oh, this is so annoying. I mean, I don't even know if I've got a boyfriend or not! How sad is that?! I'll have to think of some excuse to do with the fashion show so I can talk to JJ tomorrow. If I am his girlfriend then of course I don't need an excuse, but safest to have one anyway, because of the **AOC**. But then, maybe there will be no **AOC** at all because it will be really obvious, like maybe he will sweep me into a *Passionate Embrace*. But then, if I'm with Jules when I see him, hopefully he will know not to – I would rather let her keep thinking I am totally over him and in no way maybe perhaps actually going out with him. But then, if there is no *Passionate Embrace*, how will I know if he is my boyf or not? Even if he is, he might be too cool-acting to do a *Passionate Embrace* – which would be typical seeing as he is a boy.

Oh, how will I ever work out what he meant? It's just **TOO** confusing. I'm going to get on with my designs!

Well, I have still got the Asking Out Confusion!

And 'cos it's Friday
I'll have to put up with
it all weekend! Grrr!

I saw JJ at school in the canteen at lunch, but we didn't really talk apart from just going "Hi". I tried to hang round with him on the field afterwards too, but him and his mates were just messing around giving each other wedgies and doing fake-wrestling, so in the end I had to wander off, 'cos I felt really stupid just standing there and it wasn't exactly like I could join in, was it? (I mean, *yuck*!)

Me, Jules and Tilda went round at lunchtime selling tickets 'cos when we checked with the secretaries only 10 had been sold. We have sold 21 altogether now, which is still less than I imagined. Loads of people said they didn't even know when the show was, so I just checked the posters and some of them seem to have been accidentally taken down, probably by the cleaners or something. So we copied some more in the office and me and Jules put them back up ready for Monday.

Then after school me and Jules walked home with JJ for a bit, but when he went in the shop Jules didn't want to bother waiting for him, so I couldn't either or it might have looked suspicious. To make extra sure it didn't I said really loudly, "Yeah, we totally shouldn't bother waiting for your boring brother!" and marched off.

If me and JJ *are* going out, it's annoying that we haven't seen each other properly, and if we're not, then it's annoying that he hasn't actually *asked* me yet. Also, I don't know if he meant he was going to ask me out TO somewhere, like the cinema, or just in the going out way that we mean in the lower school where you never actually *go* anywhere but you are boyfriend and girlfriend and you get a box of Matchmakers on Valentine's Day instead of just a card.

So much has happened, but I haven't had time to write in here at all today!

Well, first of all, Tilda and Jules came over here this morning so that Mum could take all three of us round to Nan's. Sunny's dad was driving the Style School girls straight there for 11.30, and us three were planning to get there a bit before to set everything up for making the designs into reality! When Tilda arrived (she is always early and Jules is always late) we went up to my room to gather all the fashion show stuff together (including my T-shirt printing kit). When we were both in the secret of my room on our own, alone, without Jules there, I realized that I just *had* to tell Tilda about JJ or my head would most likely explode. So I made sure it really was secret by checking that Alex wasn't at the door listening through a glass, which he sometimes tends to do, and then I put

on some music for extra secretness. And then I
told Tilda all about the JJ situation and she was
just listening with her eyes going wider and wider
in amazement. When I'd finished talking (I was
quite quick in case by some miracle Jules turned
up on time) I went, "How do you think Jules will
react?"

Tilda said, "I'm guessing not well. She wasn't
too happy last time you fancied JJ. She'll probably
get in a *dark and stormy* mood with you."

"You're right," I said. "I definitely won't tell her
then."

Tilda leaped up off the bed and went, "What?
But you have to! You can't put me in this position
of knowing and then not tell our other BFF! If you
don't I'll have to tell her myself!"

I threw myself on her mercy then, which means
falling down on your knees and doing begging with
your hands clasped together. "Oh, please don't!"
I begged, claspingly. "At least till I know if there's
anything to *tell*! Like I said, we haven't even kissed

yet. And I don't even know if I've been asked out."

"I jolly well hope you *haven't*," said Tilda, with a teachery look on her face, "because JJ is far too old for you anyway, Lucy Jessica Hartley."

I was about to say, *How dare you,* and, *No, he is not,* and maybe start a pillow fight over it, but just then, Jules walked in. The music I had on must have covered up the sound of the doorbell – *yeeeeeeekkkkk!!!*

"Hey girls!" she said. "What are you doing with the door shut and music on? You must be talking about Lucy's secret boyfriend!"

I jumped up from throwing myself upon Tilda's mercy and quickly said, "No we weren't!"

Jules gave me a funny look, and I realized she hadn't heard anything and that she was just messing about so I tried to look unsuspicious. "Actually, yes we were," I said, forcing myself to smile.

Jules laughed. "Yeah, right! Course you were, Lu! Like you'd keep a secret from me!"

Tilda gave me a big eyeballing stare then, and

even though I wanted to not look at her I just couldn't not look at her, if you see what I mean. "We should get going," she said, and walked past Jules and down the stairs.

"What's up with her?" Jules asked me.

I just shrugged and said, "**PQT** probably."

(**BTW**, **Q** is our codeword for period which we made up so we could talk about it at school even if boys were there. So **PQT** is Pre Q Tension, get it? Actually, I *don't* get it, **PQT** that is, 'cos I haven't started yet, but anyway.)

I do feel a bit bad for not telling Jules about JJ, but then there's so much to do on the fashion show stuff that there's no way I can risk a **BFF** falling-out at the moment, especially when it might be over absolutely nothing. Luckily Tilda didn't tell her either. I knew she wouldn't – she's such a cool **BFF**. So anyway, going back to the outfit making—

Oh, wait, Mum is saying, "Five minutes, young lady," so I have to stop writing in here and get ready for bed.

8 mins later

Hi, I am back!

Now that Mum thinks I'm asleep I can tell you all about the fashion show stuff. (I am using a torch to see with — genius, huh?) It was so cool when we got to Nan's, 'cos she'd cleared the long workbench in her sewing room and me, Jules and Tilda laid out all the fashion show stuff on it. We put all the bits of each outfit in their own tray with the model's name on, so that nothing got lost, like this:

When the Style School girls got there I introduced Nan to them and then we all decided which trays to work on.

As we were working, us three BFF were chatting together and I had a total OH HELP! moment.

Jules was like, "Hey, guess what? I saw Suzanna yesterday and she was really upset. She heard that JJ kissed another girl."

I just said without thinking, "Well, not kissed her exactly," and then I realized Jules was giving me a weird not-understanding stare and I quickly added, "...erm, I mean, probably."

Tilda was glaring at me, and I could feel her psychicness going, *Tell her! Tell her!* and I was sending psychicness back going, NO! NO! NO!

Instead I said, "Anyway, why does Suzanna even care? She's the one who broke up with *him*, isn't she?"

"Yeah, but she's still upset!" said Jules. "No one likes to think of their ex-boyfriend immediately going off with someone else, do they?"

"S'pose not," I mumbled, and then I subtly changed the subject back to the fashion show by holding up a top and saying, "Do you think we should have two rows of silver sequins on the hem or just one?"

We had a great time all hanging out together and we got loads done. Nan ordered some pizzas at about 2 o'clock 'cos we were getting really hungry – she is just such a star, there's no way I could have done this without her.

This is what we have got so far. Liana, Jemma and Shamila's outfits are finished, apart from the beading for the neckline of Sham's top (I've brought that home with me to do first thing tomorrow morning). Jules has finished printing the boys' T-shirts and I am just going to customize them up a bit when I get to Nan's tomorrow. Apart from that we've just got Bhavan, Freya and Megan's party clothes to finish and I want to do something to Liana's jeans that she brought in to make her shopping outfit more exciting, 'cos it's a bit plain at the moment. We also had a look at everything to decide what shoes would go with the outfits. Sham is borrowing a pair from me, but most of the girls have shoes at home that will work and they're bringing them in for the final fitting on Thursday (when Nan is coming to school).

I'm going back to Nan's tomorrow, because with annoying school getting in the way, if I don't spend another whole day getting the outfits done, then we'll run out of time.

Sunday the 2nd of October

It went well at Delia-Nan's today and everything is finished apart from a few tiny bits that me and Nan-Delia are doing between us. Jules and Tilda couldn't come over again as our parents all have this thing where Sundays are family day so I had to find some other happy helpers instead, i.e. Mum and Alex. I also had Dad who was there using Nan-Delia's washing machine because he reckons he has got no clean pants left, and has worn them all and then worn them inside out. (*Yuck! I soooooo did not want to know that!*) When he said that, Mum did rolling her eyes and went to Nan, "You know, Delia, when I was a little girl I used to dream of getting married to a tall, handsome man with some grasp of personal hygiene."

"One out of three ain't bad," said Dad.

"You're only 5 foot 9, Brian!" said Mum, and she

and Nan burst out laughing and Dad pretended to sulk because he had been referring to "handsome".

Before they split up and for ages afterwards (like whole actual *months*) whenever Mum and Dad said anything slightly not-nice to each other I used to go all tense and think there was about to be a massive row (which there usually was!). But now it seems to be okay for Mum to tease Dad a bit and he doesn't really mind. Maybe now he is a successful DJ and he has got loads of fans for his radio show for students that is on in the middle of the night, he doesn't mind so much what she thinks any more. Or maybe he has just generally rediscovered his sense of humour. Anyway, I don't really care why things are better, I'm just glad they are.

Dad did try helping with the fashion show stuff by sewing up a hem, but his stitching was so upsy-downsy that in the end we had to put him on making-lunch duty, which was only really doing the veggies and keeping an eye on the chicken in the oven. But he still kept coming in to ask Nan what to do and every time he went out Mum and Nan would burst out laughing. In the end I had to tell them to stop because I thought they were being a bit mean to Dad when at least he was making an effort. (It was in fact a lovely dinner and even Mum and Nan had to admit *that* without sniggering.)

I'm so glad all the fashion show stuff is v. v. nearly done – phew! I was getting a bit worried that the models would have nothing to wear on Friday. Well, not *nothing* nothing, but you know what I mean!

Monday

Oh, dear, things aren't going very well today! First of all there was Mr. Cain's talk in lower school assembly, called *Skirt Lengths for Decency and Modesty*. He stared at me the whole time he was talking and I know he was trying to make me not do short skirts in the fashion show – well, *ha ha tough*, because we are.

We had a fashion show organizer meeting at lunchtime, and Mr. Wright let us have it in the classroom 'cos the hall was being used for country dancing club. Simon reported that the sound and lighting stuff is fine and we agreed when the different music and lights and that will come on. Jules reported that the after-show party planning is going well and her mum is making loads of cool Spanish tapas for it.

Yum

97

Tilda reported that she's arranged to get free fruit cocktails from Cool Cats café for the fashion show, as long as we mention them on the night, which I will most definitely  remember to do when I am doing the thank yous.

Tilda reported that even with our posters back up we have only sold 4 more tickets today, making a not-so-grand total of 25. When she reported this I felt my chest going all fluttery with panic again. The one thing I hadn't thought of in all the fashion show planning was: *what if people don't come?* We'll have to have a massive ticket-selling mission in the next couple of days or the whole thing will be a great big giant flop.

The teeny ticket sales are massively bothering me but I will just have to carry on and think positive. To help the thinking positive I have made a professionalistic To Do list:

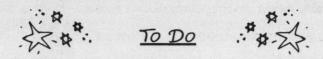

<u>To Do</u>

1. SELL MORE TICKETS!
2. Go through the final lighting and sound plans with Simon.
3. Finish the beading on Megan's top.
4. Buy some more glitter bangles from Beaujangles to go with Shamila's party look.
5. Check with Nan about how to hem up Freya's dress.
6. Kiss JJ.

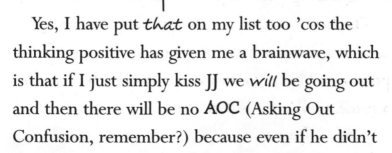

Yes, I have put *that* on my list too 'cos the thinking positive has given me a brainwave, which is that if I just simply kiss JJ we *will* be going out and then there will be no **AOC** (Asking Out Confusion, remember?) because even if he didn't actually ask me out, then a kiss would be like *me* asking *him*, if you get what I mean. **HA-HA-HAAAAAA!**

— Evil-genius laugh again!

Hang on a tic, I have to quickly do something...

I just now rang up Tilda on my mobile and told her about the Number 6 Thing on my list. I wanted her to be excited for me, but she just went all teachery again, and even though I couldn't see her face I knew there was a stricty expression on it. You could also tell by the way she was using my full name. She went, "Lucy Jessica Hartley, I really don't think you should do the Number 6 Thing seeing as JJ is still **TOO OLD** for you as I have mentioned before. Anyway, you should be more bothered about selling tickets than kissing boys at this precise moment in time, or we will have a complete crisis on our hands."

"I *am* thinking about selling tickets," I said. "I am also thinking about the Number 6 Thing to keep my positivity up."

I could just *feel* down the phone that Tilda was looking unimpressedly at me in a teachery way. "Also, you have to tell Jules because we are all a three and it's not fair if we both know and she doesn't, especially if you are going to insist on doing the Number 6 Thing, which knowing you you probably will, whatever I say," she added.

I was going to argue back, but then I just felt really annoyed about her non-supportiveness so I pretended to be in the car going through a tunnel by making whooshing noises and then hanging up, which is what you do when you want to cut someone off on your mobile without making them offended.

Tilda is right about something – I am doing the Number 6 Thing tomorrow whatever she thinks and that is that!

Oh, I am going all stomach-flippy just imagining it!

I have to go and finish putting the little sticky gems on Freya's jeans now, before I can go to bed.

I've got to be in school early in the morning to copy more posters and put them up before registration, when I am going to sell tickets in the Year 7 classes. Huh, see Tilda? I *am* v. v. bothered about tickets 'cos of this simple maths:

No tickets = no audience = no money for Oxfam = no goats.

Plus, all our hard work on the designs will be wasted. In actual fact, I can hardly *stand* to think about it! I'll have to make sure we sell loads tomorrow.

So *byeeeeeeeeee*!!!!!!

Tuesday at first break

I am quickly writing
this in the loos before
I go and do the Number 6
Thing on my list.

I just had to give Jules the slip after maths and
say I was off to see Simon about the fashion show
stuff (Tilda is in the brainy maths group, so she
wasn't with us). Actually, Jules was a bit weird just
now. When I said my fake excuse about Simon,
she went, "Anything you want to tell me, Lucy?"
and gave me a really intense glare like she was
looking through my head and into my thoughts.

I said no, puzzledly, and she went, "Fine! Then
there's nothing I want to tell *you* either!" and
stormed off! I have no idea what she was on about,
but there's no time to worry about it now. Wish
me luck with the Number 6 Thing!

Oh, URGH!
I have just had the most giant CRINGE of my life!

I am back in the loos, which is where I will most probably be living until the actual

END OF TIME

The thing that happened is – yurgh, I am really having to make myself write this – well, I spotted JJ going down that little walkway between the main school and the food science block where there is only a tiny gap and everyone tries to push through at once. It was completely in public but I had to put up with it, 'cos I knew I just had to do the Number 6 Thing and then I would be his girlfriend and all the *Asking Out Confusion* would be over.

"JJ, I…" I began, and then I felt like running away, so I made myself hurry up. I stood up on tiptoes and leaned towards him with my eyes shut. It seemed like a really long way to be leaning and I was still not getting to his lips so I opened one eye and saw that he was actually leaning backwards away from me instead of forwards like you are supposed to if someone is about to be kissing you.

So I kept leaning forwards and he kept leaning backwards and then our balance went and we both had a stagger about with flailing arms. That's when I finally realized the *Awful Truth* (argh – I am so intensely immensely dense sometimes!) that he didn't want to kiss me. Then I was in complete total mortification (which is when you are so embarrassed you want to just **DIE, BTW**).

But just then JJ took my hand and pulled me round the side of the food science block, and a few Year 7s started going "*Whoo-oo-oo-oo!*"

For a tiny moment there was a Glimmer of

105

Hope and I thought it might actually BE *whoo-oo-oo-oo*, 'cos my brain was going,

He only didn't kiss me back 'cos it was in front of loads of people and he's dragging me round the side of the food science block so no one can see us except those Year 7s who are in there finishing off making cheese straws!
Yay!

While I was still thinking that, JJ started talking. And he said—

Oh, I can hardly stand to write it down.

He said, "The thing is, Lu, it's probably best if we're just friends."

So definitely no need for going *whoo-oo-oo-oo* then.

Before I could think of anything cool to say, this stupid baby sentence started coming out of my mouth, which was, "But you said could you maybe ask me out, and I thought you maybe had." Then I went even redder and clamped my lips shut to stop any more cringiness leaking out.

JJ shrugged and looked like he'd rather be doing *anything* except having this talk with me, like even sticking his hand into a sink of poisonous lizards or wearing a pink tutu in assembly. "It's just, Suzanna came round last night and we got talking and I realized I still like her, so we've decided to get back together," he mumbled, looking at the floor.

Luckily I still had my lips clamped tight shut from before, because I managed to stop myself from shouting, "But you can't go out with **HER**, you're meant to be going out with **ME!**"

"I'll still be in the show, though," he added, like that was supposed to make me feel better.

I managed to do a shrug, and go, "Cool,

whatever." I walked shakily back to the little corridor bit and I was feeling so weird I actually had to *think* about how to even WALK (i.e. by putting one foot in front of the other) because it was like my legs had forgotten what to do.

I'm sure you have noticed this already and I don't really need to say it again, but I am *soooooo* upset, plus v. v. embarrassed! You could cook eggs on my face right now it's so hot! Plus, with the ticket sales for the show being so rubbish it just feels like everything's going wrong. I am starting to think maybe I am DOOMED.

Oh, no, that is Jules coming in. She's calling me. I'll just stay quietly in here and she'll never find—

Erk, she's looking under the door!

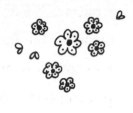
in the little doorway round
the back of the art room,
with just my journal for
company (not that I CARE!)

Oh, things just get worserer and worserer. (I
know *Mr. Walking Dictionary* Simon Driscott
would say that's not even a word, but I'm not
exactly in the mood for bothering about
grammaticulous correctness!) Maybe I really
am DOOMED!

I'll start again from where I left off writing, so
you don't miss any of the annoyingness that has
happened.

So, remember that Jules's head was sticking
under the toilet door? Well, Jules's head said a
most surprising thing, which was, "Lucy, I know
about JJ."

And just when I was thinking, **WHAAAAAAT?** a

floating voice that was Tilda's said, "I'm sorry but I told her about your crush, 'cos she told me JJ had got back with Suzanna and I was so shocked it just came blurting out."

I flung the toilet door open then, so it was lucky that Jules had moved her head out of the way.

"WHAAAAAAAAAAAAAATTTTTTT??????!!!!!!!!!!!!" I yelled, not sure who to be more moody with.

Jules was standing there with her arms folded, looking very *dark and stormy*. "Why didn't you tell me about re-fancying JJ?" she said demandingly.

I was like, "Because...but hang on, why didn't *you* tell *me* about him getting back with Suzanna?! I have just suffered a MAJOR CRINGE and you could have saved me from it!"

That's when Tilda swivelled round and looked really angry with Jules. "I told you to warn Lucy not to go up to JJ and you *didn't*! Jules, you knew I couldn't grab her myself 'cos I had to stay behind after maths! Why didn't you stop her?"

I fixed Jules with a super-moody glare. "Yeah, why didn't you stop her...erm, I mean me?" I demanded demandingly.

"Well, because you didn't tell me about any of this and..." Jules began.

Suddenly I realized that *this* was the weird thing Jules had been going on about at the start of break, that I hadn't quite got. She'd been about to tell me the JJ-loves-Suzanna news and just because I didn't tell her about re-liking him she decided NOT to tell me but instead to let me make a massive idiot of myself.

"You **KNEW** and you **LET** me make a massive idiot of myself?" I yelled.

"You kept something from me but told Tilda when we're all meant to be a three?" she yelled back.

"Well, I thought you'd tease me in front of him or get all moody about it," I yelled back (back). "But I'm glad *that* hasn't happened," I added, for sarcastic effect.

"So you don't trust me, but you trust *her!*" Jules yelled then. "Charming!"

"Maybe I shouldn't have done! Seeing as she can't keep a secret!" I yelled, giving *Tilda* my massive moody glare too.

"You shouldn't have expected me too!" went Tilda, startling me by yelling back just as loud as me and Jules were yelling.

The bell rang just then and Jules said, "Yeah, Lucy! You shouldn't have expected her to. At least someone round here knows how to be a decent **BFF**. Come on, Tilda, let's go to English on our *own*."

Jules tried to link arms with Tilda then, to do a double *dark and stormy* storming off with her, but Tilda just folded her arms and went, "No thanks, Jules. Just 'cos I think JJ is too old for Lucy, doesn't mean I agree with how you acted.

You let her go up to him for kissing purposes when you knew she would only end up looking stupid! That's not BFFness!"

"Yeah!" I said. "Come on, Tilda, let's go to English without *her*!"

"No chance!" Tilda yelled at *me* then. "I am still in a big mood with you as well, Lucy Jessica Hartley, and by the way, I know you didn't really go through a tunnel when you cut me off on the phone last night!"

Just then the door swung open and it was Mrs. Stepton clearing people out of the loos. We all just froze, staring at each other in Massive Annoyance and then Tilda stormed out and so did Jules.

I stormed after them and found them both going in different directions down the corridor, so I went back out into the playground, just to storm somewhere that they weren't storming, and I had to walk all the way round the building to get back to class.

So, to put it in that sciency way that Mrs. Stepton likes, we are in a triangle of annoyedness, like:

Me cross with them

Them cross with each other, and me

GRRRR – how could Tilda have told Jules, and how could Jules not have told me? They are *soooooo* annoying. In fact, I'm actually *glad* I'm here round the back of the art room on my own writing this and not with them!

Afternoon break

sitting on bench in playground on own.

Well, okay, maybe it is a tiny bit boring without the horrible Miss J and the annoying Miss T, and maybe I was a *teeny-weeny microscopic* bit to blame for our **BFF** falling-out-ness as well. At least I have got ticket selling to take my mind off the two meanies! I was hoping that if I sat here people would come up to me, but they haven't so I will have to go round the groups. Wish me luck!

GOOD LUCK

You will not BELIEVE what's happened

SHOCK

On the way out of school at home time I was walking down the corridor to the office and I glanced at the "Events" pinboard to see the fashion show poster and it wasn't there. Again.

I suddenly realized that it couldn't have accidentally been taken down twice by the cleaners. So someone must have taken it down on purpose.

My stomach absolutely dropped into my shoes then, and I was thinking, *Who would do something like that?* I was just utterly without words and I felt sick and trembly to think that someone could do that, especially as the fashion show is in aid of charity.

Just then, Tilda and Jules came along and found me standing there staring at the space where the poster was meant to be.

"When I was selling tickets at last break, Sam Briant's lot said they hadn't seen a poster at all," said Tilda, "and so I took them to the lunch hall to show them the one on the door and it wasn't there."

"So she told me and we've just checked and it's the same all round the school," added Jules. "They've been taken down."

"Someone's trying to sabotage the fashion show, Lucy," Tilda half-whispered.

Of course I was in SHOCKED STUNNEDNESS about this terrible news, but also I was having a moment of Best Friend Appreciation. "You two kept selling tickets even when we weren't talking to each other," I cried. "That's true BFFness! I'm sorry I didn't tell you about my crush, Jules, and I'm so sorry I got in a mood with you for telling Jules about my crush, Tilda. I shouldn't have expected you to keep it secret in the first place."

"I'm sorry too," said Jules. "I should have told you about JJ and Suzanna, Lu. Look, shall we just make up and get on with working out what on earth is going on?"

We all agreed that was the best idea, so we had a big **BFF** hug, and did the "Make friends, make friends" song, which is this stupid thing me and Jules started doing when we were five, that goes:

Make friends, make friends,
Never, never break friends,
If you do, you'll catch the flu
And that will be the end of you!

Just then, Tilda's dad poked his head round the corner and called her to the car, and she had to hurry off.

When it was just us, Jules said, "I'm really sorry about JJ, Lu, I mean, *really*. But there are plenty more fish in the sea, and by fish I mean boys who are in no way related to me."

"Thanks. I'm okay about it, kind of," I said back. "Tilda was probably right, he *is* too old for me, and plus it's all so complicated, this Asking Out business."

"And by the way, you *can* trust me," she said then. "I know I can be a bit of a bigmouth sometimes, but I would *never* be like that over something that really mattered to you, even if it is you liking my big bro."

"Thanks," I said, and I realized that I should have just trusted Jules in the first place and not decided that she would act horrible about it. "With so much to organize I don't have time to even remotely start thinking about boys anyway so it's probably for the best," I added.

Jules grinned and said, "Yeah, most likely. Right then, let's get started on saving this fashion show!"

So we made some more copies of the poster from the only one left up (in the staffroom) and put them up all round the school.

7.18 p.m.
Feel the weirdness
and mysteriosity...

HOOT

Jules just rang me and went, "The owl hoots at midnight."

I was like, "Eh?" and she was like, "It's what you say when you're doing a Secret Undercover Operation, Lu. I've been thinking, and the only way to find out who's behind this despicable sabotage is to have a **SUO**. Text Simon Driscott and Tilda and the Style School girls and get them to meet us in the little doorway round the back of the art room at oh-eight-hundred hours before school starts. Tell them all to bring their mobiles."

"But hang on, I don't know if I've got Simon's number, and what is oh-eight-hundre—" I began, confusedly.

But Jules just went, "Trust me, Lucy. Do you trust me?" like she was in a spy film.

I thought of all what had happened today, with the JJ stuff, and I knew that I could. "Affirmative," I said, trying to sound undercover-ish myself.

"Good," said Jules. Then she added, "The black crow flies over the water," which must be another Secret Mission Saying, and hung up.

I was going to ring back but I knew there was zero point. It would only get more confusing 'cos Jules likes to be mysterious. It is part of her being all Spanishly exotic, whereas I am English and I like things to be straightforward so I know what on earth is going on.

Still, I found out I do have Simon's number, from when he was doing the mobile disco at Tilda's party that I organized, and I've got Jemma's too, and she is going to text the other Style School girls to get them to come as well. Simon told me that oh-eight-hundred hours means 8 a.m., so at least I know when to turn up now.

Wednesday
at 6.12 a.m.

I have woken up v. early wondering what on earth Jules has in mind for *Operation Save Our Show*.

Now I'm awake I suppose I might as well get up and finish off the safety pins along the bottom of Jamie's T-shirt (I've cut the hem off it too, for extra grooviness). I'm doing the boys kind of funky and punky and Rock 'n' Roll for the party look, but I've put the Polaroid of JJ in a drawer so I don't have to constantly look at it and be reminded of my major CRINGE!

In computers

The bell's just gone and I'm printing out my – ahem – work to stick in here. Lucky we have still got Mr. Webb the student teacher, who just reads *What Car?* mag and lets us get on with our personal projects as long as we are quiet!

Report on: Operation Save Our Show

Secret Agents: Jules and Lucy and Tilda

(CODENAME: 3BFF4FR)

Backup: The Style School girls and Simon Driscott

Summary of ~~Maneuvers~~ ~~Manuvers~~ ~~Manoeuvres~~

Oh, you know what I mean!

0800 hours a.m.: We all met in the little doorway round the back of the art room as Jules had instructed. Jules explained to the Style School girls and Simon Driscott what's been happening with the posters. She then revealed her top secret plan, which is to secretly put the newly-put-up posters under surveillance and try to catch someone taking them down. We were assigned to one each, and we all typed the same message into our phone, which was <u>SOS! Come to XXX</u> (I don't mean we actually *put* XXX but I have written XXX down here to mean whatever our individualistic location was). Then we all swapped phone numbers and set the message to go to everyone else, so that if we caught the sabotager we could just silently press send and the message would go round to everyone and they would come running to be backup. Genius, huh?

8.12 a.m.: Everyone started coming into school and we were all in our lookout positions. I was hiding round the corner of the changing rooms in that bit which goes into the sports hall, surveiling the poster we had put up on the noticeboard there.

8.14 a.m.: Nothing happened (apart from that I surveiled the poster).

8.16 a.m.: Still nothing happened.

8.18 a.m.: *Still* still nothing happened.

8.22 a.m.: Huge great piles of nothing happened. Plus, I was getting very bored and my neck was going stiff from craning it round the corner.

8.25 a.m.: Still nothing.

8.27 a.m.: Nothing again.

8.32 a.m.: I started thinking nothing was ever going to happen and so I was about to give up and just go in the girls' loos and experiment with make-up, when...

8.35 a.m.: My mobile burst into its jazzy tune and there was the preset message. It was from Tilda, so I sprinted over to her lookout post at the science labs as fast as I could, meeting Carla and Jemma along the way. We burst into the building and found Tilda standing in the corridor with her hands on her hips and a very angry look on her face. In front of her was Gina Fulcher and in Gina Fulcher's hand was a fashion show poster. Gina Fulcher was just pushing past Tilda and making for the door when we burst through it. When she saw us she looked really startled and backed away down the corridor.

Suddenly Sunita and Lizzy and Simon Driscott came bursting in the other door and Gina was stuck. "Do not try any funny business!" I commanded. "We have you cornered."

"Yeah right, dream on, Lucy! I'm not scared of a few Year 7s and your geeky boyfriend," said Gina, with a sneer.

"Simon Driscott is not that geeky!" I shouted. "And he is most definitely not my boyfriend!"

Simon went bright red and Gina muttered, "Whatever. I'm outta here."

But then Jules arrived and it turned out Gina was a bit scared of *her*.

So, with all my backup people for protection I did an interrogation on Gina like I have seen on Police

Squad, except that I didn't have a bright lamp to shine in her face. Turns out that she's been taking the posters down because we didn't pick her to be a model, so she wants to spoil the show! I got really angry then

and told her about the kids with no goats and that.

At first she wasn't bothered, but then I could tell that she *was* bothered but that she was trying to still look *not* bothered, if you know what I mean. She promised to leave the posters alone from now on. "You'd better," said Jules, "or we'll be telling Mr. Phillips what you did."

"Like I care," said Gina, but I reckon she secretly did.

When Gina had gone sloping off, we all did high fives, and shouts of happiness, and then Mrs. Stepton came out of her science room and told us off for being noisy and sent us to our own classrooms for registration.

Mr. Phillips spotted me and asked how things were going, so I told him about the teeny ticket sales and said we'd had some trouble with the posters being taken down (but mentioning no names, i.e. Gina Fulcher!). So to help us he announced about the show in whole school assembly this morning and pointed out me and Jules and Tilda so everyone knew who to get tickets from. He's even going to ask Mr. Wright to let us go round the classes selling tickets during tomorrow morning's form time.

So even though Gina is leaving the posters alone now we have realized that time is ticking LOUDLY and we need to do all we can to sell tickets. Our crack team of Gina-busting people met up at first break and Tilda got all the leftover tickets from the school office and we split up and went round selling them. It's going really well so far. Plus, lots of people have promised to bring in money tomorrow 'cos they didn't have enough on them, so that's good too.

The assembly announcement really helped and now that people can see the posters too it's like, you know the saying about *word* getting round – well, a *word* is definitely getting round about the show and the word is FABULASTIC!

At home,
having a Wagon Wheel
of Triumph.
Amazingly...

...we have now sold all 62 tickets for the seats and we have photocopied 60 more in the office 'cos we had the **REVELATION** that people can stand as well (for only £2!), and we want to make as much money for buying goats as possible. Plus, having standers will add to the atmosphere, like at a rock concert!

I've just got everything out ready for the final fittings tomorrow and the outfits look *soooooo* cool! I can't wait to see them on the models!

Thursday the 6th

I'm seeing JJ today, for the first time since the cringe-making *happening where nothing happened* happened. Fingers crossed it goes okay!

Still Thursday,

I am just quickly writing this before science starts, while Mrs. Stepton is organizing the beakers and stuff.

Just to say that it went okay with JJ, I managed to speak normally to him and not just mumble embarrassingly while looking at my shoes. Nan came in at lunchtime and I introduced her to my fab team and also Mr. Phillips, who was there to go through all the final checks for tomorrow with us.

We pulled the stage curtains shut to make a changing room and she fitted everything on the models and did the final pinning up and adjusting. I was going round helping her and checking everything, with a load of pins in my mouth and it just felt so cool and even more like I am a *Real Actual Fashion Designer* than before. I can't believe the fashion show is tomorrow!

I thought it was going to go not okay with JJ for a minute because after we'd done the girls, the boys came in just to try on their T-shirts (we know their jeans fit and I would have been way too embarrassed to get them to change in front of me anyway – however professionalistic I am they are still **BOYS**). Suzanna came in with JJ and she was going, "Oh, Lucy, it's so great that you're doing this show for charity," and mentioning how talented I was and that.

Obviously she didn't seem to know that the rumour about JJ kissing a girl was kind of probably about me and I hope it stays that way! I feel a bit of a **CRINGE** coming on when I even *think* about the *Return of the Killer Crush*, 'cos even though I am an actual teenager now and not just a very nearly one, Tilda was right all along when she said JJ is too old for me. Not that I would ever admit that to anyone apart from my **BFF**! Anyway, I'm glad Suzanna just saw me as JJ's kid sister's **BFF**, and not his nearly-possibly-sort-of-girlfriend!

JJ has still got a problem with nervosity, though. Simon Driscott and the Geeky Minions set the stage blocks up in a catwalk so the models could have a practice walking down it in the finished clothes, and even though the girls had left and it was only him and Jamie Cousins doing it, JJ was still quaky with fear! I'm a bit worried that tomorrow when everyone is watching he'll just freak out and freeze to the spot, or even start doing the walk and then tumble into the audience with Mortal Terror. I'll have to try and work out a way of curing him — and fast!

At least the ticket sales are flying now — we have

sold 36 more of the standing-up ones by going round the classes at registration and the secretaries have sold 10 more too – so only 14 left now!

Oh, gotta go – our scientific experiment stuff is all set up and Jules and Tilda have already started. If I don't put this journal away, Mrs. Stepton will be asking to see what I'm writing and I definitely don't want⸃

Still, still Thursday,
but it is now after school.

Sorry about ending so quickly before – as you can guess, Mrs. Stepton could work out with her teachery sixth sense that I was not actually doing science and she started coming over so I had to quickly shove this journal in my bag under the bench.

Well, everything is going really well and is sorted

out for the show, except that one disaster has occurred. When I got back from school Mum had just come in from work and she made us a cup of tea (and some watered-down orange juice for Alex – weird that she doesn't just give it to him normally how it is in the carton because it's meant to be healthy, but anyway). I was babbling away about the fashion show and instead of looking excited Mum just looked really anxious, like she did when she accidentally mixed a brown sock in with my white washing and everything ended up this sort of grungy mud colour. I stopped saying about the glitter body spray I've got for the girls to wear in the party bit of the show and went, "Mum, what's up? Have you dyed all my stuff a weird colour again by accident?"

She went, "What? Oh, erm, no. It's just… Oh, Lucy, I'm so sorry, but Mr. Snellerman has refused to let me leave early for the show tomorrow."

At first I wasn't that bothered 'cos the full reality had not sunk in, and I just went, "Oh, don't worry about that, just say you're sick, that's what I usually do if I want to get out of something."

She raised her eyebrow and went, "Do you now?"

Whoops! I realized what I'd said and quickly changed it by going, "Well, *I* don't, obviously. I meant to say, this girl in my class does. But not anyone you know."

Mum's eyebrow stayed raised. "Would this be the same girl who's sweet on an older boy?" she asked.

I went really red then but luckily I managed to go, "Erm, yes it is her, but she doesn't like the older boy any more and she has realized that older boys are too old for her and that she's generally too busy to bother about boys anyway."

"Good," said Mum.

"And pleeeeeease don't say 'sweet on'," I added.

So I thought everything would be okay about her bunking off to do the make-up but apparently it is Not That Simple. She can't pretend to be sick now she's told Mr. Smellyman (as I am now calling him) it's the fashion show or he'll know she's not really ill and she'll get in loads of trouble. And she can't just come anyway or she risks losing her job. Mr. Smellyman is extra mean because when Mum first asked him about having the afternoon off he said he thought it would be fine, but when she just checked to make sure, he changed his mind and said that there is loads of work she has to finish by the end of Friday and how it is Not Fine after all.

Well, when I realized she wouldn't be able to come, my stomach did a horrible dropping thing, but I made myself look normal and managed to mumble, "It's okay." I mean, I know Mum really *really* wants to come and be the make-up artist and I also know that Mr. Smellyman is a total Prehistoric Idiot who does not understand one bit about the needs of working mothers who have daughters who are doing vitally important fashion shows in aid of charity. But a bit of disappointment must have showed in my face, and maybe in the way that I was still stirring my tea even though the sugar had dissolved into it about two minutes before, because Mum said, "You know what, Lu? It's not okay! It's not *fair*! Your dad gets to do a job he loves while I'm stuck working for a Prehistoric Idiot, as you call him, who won't even give me one afternoon off to support my daughter at her first fashion show. It is NOT OKAY AT ALL! Right, I'm going in the bath to RELAX!"

And with that, she stormed out of the kitchen, slopping her tea as she went. I knew she was really upset because she didn't even bother to get a bit of kitchen roll and wipe up the spill even though she is always telling me and Alex off for leaving the mess on the floor when *we* drop stuff.

Poor Mum! It'll take about a gallon of Radox to relax her the mood she's in, and I think she only has half a bottle left. And also, poor me! How on earth am I going to manage without a make-up artist?

I suppose I'll have to ask Mum if I can borrow

her kit and try to do the make-up myself while also being the producer and the designer. **Eeekkkkkkk!** Quel nightmaro! But the show must go on.

Oh, hang on, the phone is ringing—

46 minutes later

𝒟ad just rang, to ask me how everything is going. I said, *Fine, thanks,* and told him the good stuff and didn't mention Mum and the make-up thing 'cos she was standing right there towelling her hair. I don't want her to think she has given me a major crisis, 'cos of it not being her fault. Mum said she wanted a quick word with him after I'd finished, and when I handed her the phone I was going to ask when tea would be ready, but she still looked so unrelaxed even after her bath that I decided not to. I just grabbed a couple of Baby Bels out of the fridge instead to keep me going, and when I left the kitchen, Mum was sounding really annoyed and saying, "No, I can't come… Well, of course I wanted to be involved, Brian, but…" down the phone.

Now I'm going to finish making the cool necklace I designed to go with Liana's party outfit. It's like:

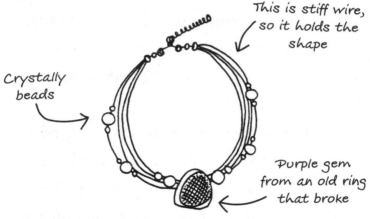

This is stiff wire, so it holds the shape

Crystally beads

Purple gem from an old ring that broke

I might even do one for Bhavan too, 'cos it would go so well with her spangly top. Hopefully concentrating on something else will stop me worrying about not having a make-up artist too!

Bye!

7.20 p.m.

Well, it's nearly an hour later and I've finished both necklaces and I just decided to go and get a hot choc and maybe dare ask when tea might be ready and weirdly I found that Mum is still on the phone. I came sort of halfway down the stairs and saw her sitting on the floor in the hall by the phone table, leaning her wet hair against the radiator.

First I thought that Dad must have rung off and then she'd rung Gloria or someone, 'cos Mum and Dad only ever talk on the phone for about 0.6 seconds to arrange about picking me and Alex up, etc. I was about to go down, when I heard Mum say, "But that's the thing, Brian, I've only just worked out what I really want…"

Something in my Female Intuition (which I have been developing by using the cool Teen Witch Kit that Tilda and Jules got me) told me not to go downstairs and interrupt her. But how weird that she is still talking to Dad. Now I'm back up here I may as well take my mind off being mega-hungry by working out what to do about JJ's nerves.

I know – mentioning my Teen Witch Kit has just given me the idea that there might be some sort of potion or spell or something for nervosity that I can use.

A bit later

Well, I have had a look and found a few things in my Teen Witch Kit. Mum is off the phone now and making the dinner (thank goodness, I'm soooooo hungry!) so I'll go downstairs and see if we've got any of the anti-nervosity stuff…

Hello again!

We have got:

* Camomile Tea
* Lavender Oil
* Rescue Remedy

(Luckily Mum has this in her handbag. She reckons she needs it for when "you kids" are driving her a bit mad. Now that I am a teenager and I am massively mature, she obviously only means Alex!)

Mum also suggested *Deep Cleansing Breaths* for JJ's nervosity, which she likes to do in traffic jams and when me and Alex are fighting over the remote control. And also, in my Teen Witch Kit it says to do *Positive Affirmations*, which are these sayings that you repeat over and over that make your brain change from thinking something is *scary* to thinking it is *fun*. None of the affirmations in my kit were exactly right so I have made up my own one for JJ, which is:

> *I am confident at modelling and I love being on the catwalk with 122 people all watching me.*

Good, huh? That should definitely make him relax.

Guess what?! We have now sold all our standing tickets too! I wanted to photocopy some more in the office after school today, but Mr. Phillips said no, because of too many people being a hazard (not that they mind squashing about 8 million of us in there for inter-school country dancing but as he is the Head I didn't dare mention that).

I can't believe the fashion show is sold out! That's *soooooo* amazing! I just really hope everything goes well tomorrow.

Oh, Mum is calling me down to help set the table now. I bet *Real Actual Fashion Designers* never have to do table setting because they only ever eat out in posh restaurants where you have loads of different knives and forks and that (including that weird special kind of knife you get for eating fish) and where if you spill something on the cloth they wipe it up with a specially designed little hoover.

Gotta go!

Friday the 7th of October

~~This is meant to be my equations~~
~~rough working out paper but I'm too~~
~~excited to think about maths!~~

This morning I checked and double-checked
and then triple-checked that I'd got
everything for the fashion show (I really hope
I have!). Mum dropped me off here and helped
me get all the stuff out of the car and put it
in the office, which is where we're keeping it till
after school. When she said goodbye she
looked really sad, and she kept saying sorry
she couldn't come and everything. Poor Mum!
I really, really wish she could make it to the
show.

Even with the make-up artist problem, I
am so excited about the show I am having

145

to stop myself bursting into giggles, and I don't even dare look at Jules and Tilda, in case we start each other off, which we _have_ this habit of doing. Only 5 hours and 15 mins to go!

Make that 5 hours and 14 mins!

Hang on, it is now 5 hours and 13 mins!

Gotta go, Tilda's nudging me, meaning Teacher Alert!

146

I know this is very late for me to still be in bed, but we didn't get back here from the after-show party till nearly 11. I was going to write in here all about the fashion show when we got back last night, but by the time I got in bed I was completely totally tired out to beyond the point of exhaustion and I just fell asleep the minute my head hit the pillow (I always thought that was just a phrase but now I know it can happen in actuality).

I am sitting up in bed with my tea and I've finished eating some toast and jam that Alex brought up for me (**BTW**, please don't start thinking that he must be a really nice bro, 'cos I had to pay him 20p per slice!). I just really want to blurt out all the fab fashion show stuff at once, but I will *make* myself start at the beginning and say

147

everything in the right order and give you all the fab details and juicy info.

It was so cool 'cos me, Jules, Tilda, Simon Driscott and the Geeky Minions (I mean, the Charming Friends) got off geography half an hour early so we could set things up for the fashion show. Simon and the ~~GMs~~ CFs put the stage blocks out to make the catwalk and Jules arranged the chairs, while me and Tilda stuck the decorations up on the walls. We put up streamers and balloons so it looked like a party and we had paper cups for the drinks that Tilda's dad has bought us that said "party" on as well, and a "party" paper tablecloth for the drinks table. The dinner ladies are bringing the fruit cocktail that Cool Cats has donated up at 4.15, ready for when people start arriving, but we laid all the little umbrellas and swizzly stirring sticks and that out on the table first. Mr. Phillips came to check on us and said everything looked really good – so that was cool.

When the bell went, me, Jules and Tilda all had a **BFF** hug together with excitement (we tried to pull Simon in too, but he had some urgent fiddling with the sound system to do). The models and the Style School girls all arrived in the hall really quickly and so we left SD and the **GMs** to sort out the *technologicality* while us girls took them to the dressing room.

The dressing room was just the classroom nearest to the stage door of the hall, across the corridor, which is 10B's room. It didn't look anything like a dressing room at first, but once we'd drawn the blinds and put the lights on, and got the mirror on wheels in out of Nan's car (she'd just arrived too), and all the clothes were hung up on a rail brought up from the cloakroom and the make-up and hair stuff was laid out on different desks, it did start to look quite like one.

The girls said they wouldn't change with Jamie Cousins and JJ there (I don't blame them!), but they didn't need to worry – the minute the boys saw so much girly stuff in one room they bolted out and said they would change in the loos! There was no way they were letting us put make-up on them or do anything jazzy with their hair anyway! I gave JJ all my remedies (the camomile tea was still warm in its flask – well, warm-*ish*) and told him what to do with them. When I told him the affirmation I'd made up he looked really freaked out, so I said to ignore that and just concentrate on drinking the herby tea and smelling the lavender oil.

When we'd helped Nan bring all her stuff in too, somehow it was only 45 minutes till the show, so we got straight to work! While everyone was busy doing stuff, Nan called me over to the clothes rail. She handed me one of the tops and said, "I've just added a finishing touch to everything." I held it up and looked and at first I couldn't see what she'd added but then I noticed it – she'd sewn on a label that said:

"You're a designer, so you should have your own label," she said, grinning.

I was completely speechless with wonderment (v. unusual for me!!!!) and all I could do was give her a massive hug. She's sewn *Totally Lucy* labels into everything – she said she got this company to make them for her. How amazingly cool is that?

You are probably thinking, *Wow, there could not be anything more amazing than having your very own fashion label*, but then something even *more* amazing happened. I was just buzzing around everywhere checking the accessories and the hair and wondering how on earth I was going to get all the models' make-up done in 36 minutes, when guess who burst in?

It was Mum!

Of course, I was in total **GOBSMACKED FLABBERGASTATION** and I was saying, "How are you possibly here?" and stuff like that.

Mum said, "I spent the whole morning feeling so angry about not being able to come that I just decided to leave early without permission. Right, who do I need to do first?"

Wow. How cool is Mum for doing that?!

Beamingly, I introduced her to the girls and she started work on Bhavan's make-up. There was so much going on in that 36 minutes that I cannot possibly describe it all in words or my hand will be aching till about next Wednesday, so I will just draw some quick pix to show you.

My fab label!!!

Freya having her hair and make-up done

Me madly rushing around

Jemma getting
her hair done

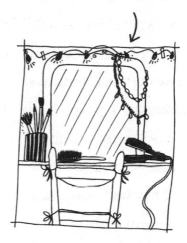

The cool make-up
area we made

At about 4.22 Shamila popped to the loo and
when she came back she said how loads of people
were queuing to get in the hall and how cool it
looked with Simon's lighting and the music and
that. So then after I'd finished sorting out Freya's
earrings I couldn't resist going to have a look for
myself. I went in the stage door and peeked
through the curtains into the hall. They were
letting people in by then, and Tilda was striding
around with her clipboard talking to them and

showing them to the drinks table and that. The lights were flashing purple and pink and the music was playing and it all looked so **AMAZING** and all these people were here waiting for the show and I suddenly realized what a big thing I was doing and I felt like I needed some of JJ's anti-nervosity remedies myself! I walked back to the dressing room on trembly legs and—

Oh, dratification! Mum is telling me to get in the shower, just as I was getting to the best bit too! So please excuse me for about 6 mins, but then I will be back to tell you something even more completely amazing than Nan making me my own labels or Mum turning up. In fact, it was *soooooo* amazing that I could hardly even believe it myself!

Sorry, that took a bit longer than I thought 'cos
I decided to use Mum's Papaya Deep Conditioner
on my hair and then when I dried it it went all
really floppy with being in such good condition
and I had to borrow her styling spray to spruce it
up again, but anyway, my hair problems are not the
point. The point is that I've got something v. v.
fabulicious to tell you about what happened next
at the fashion show!

We were just about ready to get the models into
the line-up, which is where they get in the order
that they are going onto the catwalk and we check
and make sure their hair and clothes and make-up
all look right, when Dad knocked and popped his
head round the door.

I went over and was waiting for him to say
something and he was just standing there saying
nothing but absolutely staring at Mum. Mum was

busy touching up Megan's eyeshadow while showing Sunny how to blot Freya's lipstick. I went, "Yes, Dad, Mum is here, now what's up?"

He said someone was here to see me and could she come in?

Well, I could not *believe* who walked in and I was in complete FLABBERGASTED GOBSMACKEDNESS wondering if I was imagining it!

It was Stella Boyd, the designer whose fashion show I had modelled in at London Fashion Week! Mum rushed over and hugged her and did that "mwah mwah" kissing-on-the-cheek thing that grown-ups do and she was going, "Stella, thank you so much for coming!" Stella gave me a big smile and said, "You came to my show, Lucy, and now I've come to yours!" I didn't say anything because of being so FLABBERGASTED AND GOBSMACKED so Mum said, "When you decided to put on this show, Lu, I thought I'd send Stella a ticket. I was sure she'd be far too busy to come, so I didn't mention it to you because I didn't want to get your hopes up. But she has!"

I was still not saying anything so Stella and Mum did that politeness competition adults do where one says, "Thank you so much for coming," and the other goes, "Really, it was no trouble," and then the first person goes, "Well it was very kind of you," and that goes on for up to half an hour. Finally after about 12 seconds I found my voice and thanked Stella for coming myself and then showed her the outfits. She really loved them, and she was also telling the *Style School* girls how good the hair and nails and accessorizing was and she went absolutely mad over Mum's make-up designs. Then she handed me a bag with her name on the side and in it was a top. She said it was from her latest collection and that I could auction it off for the charity at the end of the show, too! Then she wished us all luck and went to sit down, and I was just left standing there in *shocked stunnedness* wondering if I'd dreamed the last 5 and a half minutes.

Dad's head popped back round and he said,
"Lu, everyone's here." He had his
video camera ready and as

I led the line of models to
the stage door he hurried
round to the main hall so he could video the show.
My heart was pounding really hard as I gave Simon
the cue to start the catwalk music and change the
lights. (I had to just do a thumbs up, which is not
as good as having a headset, but still!)

I really wanted to watch the show, but I had to
race backstage to be ready for when the models
came back and needed help changing into their
second outfits. After a couple of minutes Jemma
and Megan came running in, talking really fast
about how fab it was, and me and Mum and Carla
helped them get changed and sent them out again.
When Shamila and Freya came back Nan and
Lizzie helped them and then everyone helped the
last two while I checked that JJ and Jamie were
okay changing in the corridor. They were high

fiving and going "Whooo!" and I told them to stop mucking around and hurry up with getting ready, but secretly I was pleased that my *Anti-Nervosity Remedies* had worked!

Then we did a second line-up in the corridor and I checked everyone over. Mum sprayed body glitter on the girls as they went by and I just had to ask Lizzie to grab the cool little sequin bag that Liana was meant to be carrying from the rail and then they were off. This time as the stage door opened and they all went through to the hall, I followed them. The disco music was pounding and the lights were whizzing round the room. The bits I got to see from hiding backstage looked amazing – the girls all remembered the *hip, hip, head* bit and the boys looked really *really* cool.

When all the models had done their walk they all went back on again together, and everyone was clapping and cheering. As she went on, Jemma grabbed my arm, and I was like, "Eek! Let go!" but she said, "The designer always comes out at the end," and dragged me onto the catwalk!

Well, it's good that she is very strong because I'm so happy I went out there! In fact, I can honestly tell you that it was about the best moment of my life so far! Everyone was clapping and going "Whoooo!" and I did a bow and then I did that thing of holding my arms out and clapping towards the models to thank them too.

Finally the clapping died down and I was left there realizing I had to say something! I started with that thing you say at the beginning of speeches, which is "My lords, ladies and gentlemen, unaccustomed as I am to doing speeches, I would just like to thank..." and then I said everyone who was involved in the fashion show, and I even remembered to say, "Simon Driscott and his team of lighting and sound engineers" instead of "Simon Driscott and his team of Geeky Minions" (phew!). Mr. Phillips came onstage then and said thank you to me, and then he did the auction for the Stella Boyd top.

Can you believe that Mr. Cain joined in the bidding for the top, for his wife? (And can you believe that someone with Style has married him!?!) Jemma's mum bid the most in the end though – £145! (I mean, £145 – for a TOP! That really is *catwalk crazy*! But still, it is all more for charity!)

Mr. Phillips did the maths so I didn't have to – phew! – and then said, "So now in total the fashion show has raised £451!"

I am still so **GOBSMACKED AND FLABBERGASTED** about that I might have to write it again.

£451.00!!!

Everyone exploded into even more clapping, and then suddenly, just like that, it was over and everyone was chatting and getting their coats on. It all went so quickly, and I wished we could magically go back in time to 3 p.m. and do the whole thing again.

When everyone had gone, we cleared up the dressing room (it was so strange when it turned back into a normal classroom again, and you wouldn't know anything amazing had happened there) and we helped Nan pack all the stuff into her car. Simon and the ~~Geeky Minions~~ Charming Friends and Dad cleared up the hall while Jules's parents headed home to take the cling film off the party food ready for us. Of course, we did invite Stella Boyd to the party but she had to be back in London by 10 for a nightclub opening – how glam-tastic is that?!

Gotta go now, Mum's giving me a lift round Jules's. Tilda's coming over too and we have to clear up seeing as it was our party.

I'm back from Jules's

I'm feeling tired after all the clearing up, and from being up late last night (though of course I am never admitting that to Mum!) so I will tell you the best bits of what happened at the party as a list:

1. Because of Jules's family being Spanish, we had cool drinks (which were sangria for the adults and fruit punch for the teenagers and children) and fab food, which was two absolutely massive paellas full of all things like chicken and fish and rice and peppers and peas and *everything*. They were really yummy, and we had loads of baguettes to go with it, plus the usual crisps and stuff you get at English parties.

2. While we were having our food, Dad plugged in the video camera and after fast forwarding through a bit he didn't realize was on there

of him doing air guitar in his pants (urgh, thanks Dad for embarrassing me in front of everyone I know) the fashion show came on. It was so cool to see it all properly. I would say specific things about what looked good but to be honest everyone looked amazing and they all did such a great job of the modelling!

3. After we'd finished eating, Jules put some salsa music on and her mum and dad tried to give everyone a dancing lesson – it was so funny, like playing Twister to music. It was even more tricky 'cos I somehow ended up with Simon Driscott as my partner and he has absolutely zero sense of rhythm. I did stand on his actual toes a few times too, but it was his fault for leaving them in the wrong place, where my feet were supposed to be! Jamie Cousins danced with Tilda – he is v. v. brave 'cos her stricty dad was watching, and he has a No Boys rule. Mum ended up dancing with

164

Dad (she said it was to save him inflicting his clumsiness on anyone else). And they spent the whole time having a funny argument about who was going to lead.

4. After that we put some normal music on and did normal dancing where you don't crush anyone's toes and that was fun too, especially when me, Jules and Tilda made up this fab dance routine to the Sugababes.

At Jules's just now, we went on the Oxfam website to order the goats 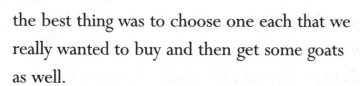 and we found so many other good things that we decided the best thing was to choose one each that we really wanted to buy and then get some goats as well.

I picked a toilet for my thing. I know that sounds weird, but toilets are important not just

for doing *you know what* in, but for having
somewhere to go and hide when you have
got yourself into a completely cringe-making
situation.

Jules chose a girls' club, which is like an after-
school youth club but just for girls, so that **BFF** can
meet and learn important stuff. That's so cool 'cos
when we are having our secret **BFF** meetings in the
little doorway round the back of the art room we
can think of the girls in the club Jules chose having
fun too! Tilda decided on care of an orphan for
the simple reason that she is so nice and caring
and loves babies. Then she did the calculating and
worked out that we could also buy 12.8 goats. All
three of us were like *wow*, 'cos that is loads! Of
course, you can't actually *get* .8 of a goat, so
Jules's mum said she would chip in the extra £4 so
we could get another whole goat, which makes 13
goats!

So here's our final list, written by Tilda, which I
am sticking in as a souvenir:

List Of Things We Are Buying For The Kids

Care for an orphan – £50

A girls' club – £63

A toilet – £30

13 goats – £24 x 13 = £312

Total = £455.00

Mum said she'll put all the money into her bank for us on Monday and then write us a cheque to send in (it would cost masses to send the actual money through the post 'cos a lot of it is £1 coins and 50ps), so that's cool.

Monday morning

I am sitting here writing
this while chewing my
Boring Hamster Bedding cereal.

It seems so weird that everything is back to
normal and that I'm just going to school in a
normal way with no fashion show to organize.
Well, actually, not everything is back to normal.
One thing is completely different. The different
thing is that Mum is sitting opposite me calmly
spreading marmalade on a piece of toast. She
never usually just eats breakfast while doing
nothing else. She usually tries to touch up her nail
polish at the same time and ends up with crumbs
in it.

I said, "Mum, why aren't you running around
madly getting ready for work? You're already in
trouble with Mr. Smellyman, and even though I
don't like him and it serves him right you bunked

168

off on Friday, I don't want you to get sacked."

"I can't get sacked, I already resigned," said Mum, and poured herself another cup of tea from the pot.

I was going, "What?"

And she said, "I had a talk to your dad about it when he dropped you and Alex back from the park yesterday."

I was staring at her with my eyeballs popping almost actually *out* and going, "Dad??"

"Yes, he's not entirely useless, regardless of the impression he gives," she said calmly. "With him doing so well at the radio station now, he can give me the child support money he owes, and pay a bit more on top of that. So I'm going to find a nice little part-time job while I retrain that doesn't involve working for a Prehistoric Idiot."

Then I was going, "Retrain as what?"

Mum smiled, like I had said something funny, and went, "Can you really not guess?"

Then I realized. She is going to become a make-

169

up artist! *My mum!* How amazingly cool is that?! She'll get me backstage at all the fashion shows all over the world and we'll get given loads of free make-up and we'll probably have to move to somewhere cool like London and everything!

I got so excited saying all this while still trying to chew my **BHB** cereal that Mum had to bang me on the back. When I had recovered she said, "Don't get too carried away, Lu. It'll probably be weddings and local events at first, but, if I work hard, maybe I really *could* do fashion shows and, well anyway, it's fun to dream, isn't it?"

Yes, it certainly is!

How amazing that I have inspired my own actual mum to follow her dreams!

And I have realized that I have also followed *my* dreams – I have put on my own actual fashion show! I can't believe it started with me moaning about this **BHB** cereal that is sitting in front of me right now and ended up in us having a cool fashion show and getting 13 goats and a toilet and a girls'

club and care for an orphan for charity! It just shows, you can do absolutely anything with fab **BFF** and a great family behind you!

Gotta go – Mum is saying that just because she's going to spend the morning in her dressing gown researching make-up artist courses and looking in the paper for part-time jobs, that doesn't excuse me from going to school! Boo!

So I'll say *byeeeeeeeeeeeeeeeeeeeeeee* for now, and don't forget, girls – when you follow your dreams, who knows what can happen!

Lots and lots and lots of love from

Lucy
Jessica
Hartley.

Lucy Jessica Hartley's
Cringe Quiz

What's your CRINGE-O-METER rating?
Are you a magnet for embarrassing
scenarios? Take my fab quiz to find out!

1. You have to do a reading in assembly.
Do you...
A) Do the whole thing brilliantly.
B) Have a shaky start then do the whole thing
   brilliantly.
C) Think you did the whole think brilliantly...
   until about 103 people come up afterwards to
   inform you that your skirt was tucked into your
   knickers the whole time.

2. Which of these salad-y things do
   you prefer:

A)   B)   C)

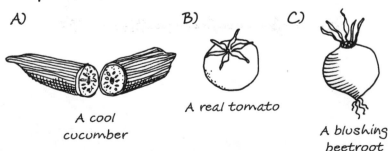

A cool   A real tomato
cucumber   A blushing
                                beetroot

3. You're strutting up the high street in your special-occasion high heels and there's a banana skin on the pavement. Do you:

A) Pick it up and put it in the bin, thinking *tut, tut, people really shouldn't drop litter!*

B) Skid on it and land in a heap — but then get up, brush yourself off and carry on walking.

C) Go flying and land in a knicker-flashing bundle of blushes right beside your crush and his annoying mate, who then photographs the occasion.

Now, turn over to get your results...

Mostly As:
Cringe-o-meter rating 2 - Serene Queen!
Lucky you – you seem to glide through life with perfect poise. But beware – that massivo cringe could be just round the corner!

Mostly Bs:
Cringe-o-meter rating 6 - Average Girl!
Well, embarrassingness gets us all sometimes, but when blushes do come knocking on your door, you know how to carry on smiling through the shame!

Mostly Cs:
Cringe-o-meter rating 10 - Princess of Cringe!
Like me, you are a magnet for cringes – but hey, look on the bright side, at least you can laugh at yourself and you're always ready with the sympathy when your **BFF** have blushes too!

Totally Secret Info about Kelly McKain

Lives: In a small flat in Chiswick, West London, with a fridge full of chocolate.

Life's ambition: To be a showgirl in Paris 100 years ago. *(Erm, not really possible that one! – Ed.)* Okay, then, to be a writer – so I am actually doing it – yay! And also, to go on a flying trapeze.

Star sign: Capricorn.

Fave colour: Purple.

Fave animal: Monkey.

Ideal pet: A purple monkey.

Biggest cringe: I'm not telling you that! But I can say that it was a 10 on the cringe-o-meter scale!

Fave hobbies: Hanging out with my BFF and gorge boyf, watching *Friends*, going to yoga and dance classes, and playing my guitar as badly as Lucy's dad!

Find out more about Kelly at
www.kellymckain.co.uk

For Matt, for everything, with love. xx
Thanks to Jemma Vater for all the
inside info. xx

First published in the UK in 2007 by Usborne Publishing Ltd., Usborne House, 83-85 Saffron Hill, London EC1N 8RT, England. www.usborne.com

Illustrations by Vici Leyhane.

The name Usborne and the devices ♈ ⊕ are Trade Marks of Usborne Publishing Ltd.

A CIP catalogue record for this book is available from the British Library.

JFMAMJJAS ND/07
ISBN 9780746080184
Printed in Great Britain.